The Riddle
of
Genesis County

The Riddle
of
Genesis County

BY LYNNE DOYLE

HOUGHTON MIFFLIN COMPANY BOSTON
1958
The Riverside Press Cambridge

*For my parents
and Nelson Algren*

*For there is hope of a tree, if it be cut down,
that it will sprout again, and that the tender
branch thereof will not cease.*

*Though the root thereof wax old in the earth,
and the stock thereof die in the ground;*

*Yet through the scent of water it will bud,
and bring forth boughs like a plant.*

*. . . But his flesh upon him shall have pain,
and his soul within him shall mourn.*

JOB 14: 7–10, 22

ACKNOWLEDGMENT is gratefully given to Vera Bethel, Quin Ream, Dana Eynon, Gerald Giving, Larry Fitzgerald, and Ken Hall for their early faith, to Dr. Roland Wolseley and Julia Braun Kessler for their encouragement, to my mother for her help, and to the family of the late Ross Lockridge, Jr., for permission to use his concepts.

CONTENTS

PART ONE

Myra

. . . For Genesis County has no surveyed bound-
aries in time or space, where yet haunt musical
and strange names of mythical people lost forever; it holds within itself both fantasy and
truth. Hunt for it in Indiana not to find it, but
find instead the delights of the searchers, and if
in the search you find yourself, you will solve the
riddle of . . .

MYRA

What Creature Is It That in the Morning of Its Life . . . ?

WHY DOES Indiana produce so many writers? I don't know. But for some reason I can describe only as instinct, I began to keep, at the printing age of seven, my writer's notebook. At ten I was lanky, bird-legged and awkward. My long red hair fell with the consistency of a cedar mop around my pigeon-bladed shoulders. My shroud of freckles added nothing of beauty. Was it in trying to write that I sought to make up for being such an ugly duckling?

Long had I suffered with the poems of Elizabeth Browning and laughed and cried with *Little Women*. Books were introduced to us by my parents who read aloud to Butch, my younger brother, and me. My mother's hobby was writing for the church; through such writing a correspondence with other writers flourished. One Irish poet wrote his letters with such beauty that I became charmed by what feelings people could create with words. My notebook's first crude girlish scrawls have faded in the past years, but the story of my writing struggles in my attempt to solve the Riddle of Genesis County, blurred with motion and green with life, is still vivid.

There are many riddles asked in Genesis County. The answers hide. What is success and failure? Have I learned that success and failure can change opinion and result, but never truth? Will Time, that tool of experience, teach me to change my opinion of what truth is? Will my search prove that the Raintree, called by my family "The Genesis Tree," was actually a descendant of the Tree of Life from the Garden of Eden? Will the search end with my hands empty but my heart full?; for this I know: The answer to the riddle is here for those who are willing to search for it.

Maybe this is why, at sixteen, I attempt to write, attempt to solve this mystery at all. By going back into the past to fit together the stray pieces of the lives of people I have known — especially those who sought to preserve Indiana's last Genesis Tree for its mythical interpretation — I shall find Truth and what holds humanity together in this mysterious brotherhood. For all these neighbors and relatives — Cosey Walters, George Dillen Hawroth, Stubby Wakefield, and Preacher Brother Gorby — are as much a part of me as they are a part of the Riddle of Genesis County. All had one thing in common. All sought an elusive condition called *happiness*.

Butch and I live with our parents here in Genesis County, Indiana. My tall, fair, and handsome father works on the railroad. If I asked my mother what she did, she would answer: "I keep busy looking after people so that they will have time to look after me."

Our nearest town is Jakeyville, once a coal miner's boom town, where King Black Diamond has been dethroned in favor of King Petty Politics, and where hangers-on continue to whistle in the dark. For this reason Jakeyville is unique in a state known for its writers, its high taxes, and its politics. Such old landmarks, fading fast, are rare in this time of Change. Our town is bisected by a state road which winds past buildings, some empty of all but the ghosts of past splendor and legends, buildings with fronts as false as the faith that a long-awaited boom will restore youth once more to the town's defeat-wrinkled countenance. But don't waste time looking for a stalwart son who will admit this truth! The town tried to keep the number of churches and saloons on an even-steven basis, but the fight was lost long before the first shot was "fired-in-the-hole." The taxes get higher for those who remain, but as for politics, that's what makes the people love the town, I guess. Around election time our candidates outdo each other in backslapping exercises. Each party rallies staunchly behind its candidate, swearing that chaos and bitterness will follow if the opposition wins. A make-believe hatred hides in knowing looks and turned up collars as they pass each other on the street the day before election. But afterward the politicians, win or lose, meet

each other across cups of cold coffee at the drugstore to divide
the spoils evenly. One cigar chewer grudgingly rises to place his
nickle in the juke box, grins, and says: "Just wait till next time."
Yet instead of going back to work, he hangs on a while longer,
afraid to leave for fear of being called a poor loser.

My great-grandfather, affectionately known as the "Fiddlin'
Man," once tried to farm the land carved from the clay. He was as
much a failure at farming as at his other economic attempts, but
when his name is mentioned people smile. This would have pleased
him. He left little of value except a book of psalms and hymns
that had been carried into Genesis County by Johnny Appleseed;
the book was my treasure that I worshiped like a golden calf.
On the flyleaf the Fiddlin' Man had written the riddle: *What
creature is it that in the morning of its life . . . ?* Long ago this farm
had been sold to the state; it has become part of the park, Shakamak.

There are those who will argue that Genesis County did not
exist here near the great Hoosier Heartland. Those doubters
shook their heads like laid-by vegetables of the Lord, crowded
into pew-cratings on the Sabbath, to murmur together about
Genesis County and the myths which a geologist, George Dillen
Hawroth, collected about the Genesis Tree. When I was nine, the
reason for this gossiping bothered me.

I found myself asking many questions with no answers. "Why
did George Dillen Hawroth, a railroader's son, search out and re-
tell the Genesis Tree myths in the first place? Why did he die?
Was it true what the gossips whispered? Had he come so close to
discovering the answer to the Riddle of Life, the secret of life and
death, that a jealous, cautious God struck him down before he
could share his discovery?"

But when I asked these questions, I was told, "Oh, Myra, you're
too young to understand," an answer that served only to whet my
curiosity. Had George Dillen Hawroth, a distant cousin of both
my parents, found the place where the Tree of Life, the tree of good
and evil like the one forbidden to Eve, grew? Would his discovery
have proved that Eden was originally in Indiana? If so, where
was this place? Could I too find it?

My only way to learn, then, was to ask. My search began that summer afternoon as Mother sat on the back porch steps. She was sorting out some of my outgrown anklets to give to another child whose family lived in the old, faded shacks near the edge of Jakeyville. The heat of the listless, sultry day pasted her auburn hair into damp ringlets on her forehead. In my awkward way I plopped down on the bottom step.

"All these people talking, Mother. Is it true? Do you think Cousin George was on the verge of solving the riddle about the Tree of Life?"

Mother shook her head the way she does when she has lost patience with me. "Oh, that again. I can see you won't quit till I answer."

When I nodded my head, she shook hers. A bee from the honey-suckle circled her head, then flew away to disappear in the sun.

Mother waited a while, as if twice measuring and weighing her words, before she answered. "To be honest, Myra, no. I don't think George made a material discovery. People loved him and liked to listen to the tales he told about our county. Facts got exaggerated, since all of us look for happiness."

"But people say he might have proved that the Genesis Tree is the one from the Garden of Eden," I offered.

"The story Cousin George searched for is as old as time itself. Many people have tried to discover the Tree of Life. You know your Bible, Myra. In the account in Genesis, after Adam and Eve had sinned, God said: *Behold, the man is become as one of us, to know good and evil; and now, lest he put forth his hand, and take also of the tree of life, and eat, and live for ever . . .*

"For that reason He sent man out of Eden. The Bible doesn't say that God destroyed the Tree of Life. So that's why people like George continue the search for it; each hopes that he will find happiness as a reward. But George didn't have to look for the secret of happiness; he carried it with him."

"If how to live forever is such a secret, is happiness a secret too?"

"Is this information for your diary-notebook or just for you?" Her laugh was teasing. "Either way, happiness is no secret. George

was the happiest of all my cousins because he kept the rules
for happiness. He was curious; he was godly; and he practiced
the simple creed: It's impossible to give away all you possess."

"It's *impossible to give away* all you possess!" Her favorite saying made me angry once more; I waited to marshal my thoughts
before attacking with my right flank of reason. "That creed of
yours is stupid," I began. "If you give away all you possess, soon
you will have nothing left for yourself. For me, too. Just for the
sake of argument, supposing I gave away all the dimes in my bank;
soon it would be empty."

"Not all wealth is in banks," she said as she rolled up a pair
of pink anklets. "Supposing you took all the dimes out of your
bank and gathered up all your most precious possessions into a
big heap. If you gave your cousin Dinah that blue sweater, and
the silver bracelet she admires, what would Dinah do?"

I played the game taught to me by my grandmother, the game
of acting as if I had magically been changed into someone else.
"Oh, Dinah would be tickled-pink happy because she can't find
any more just like them!"

"And what would happen if you gave your grandmother's
china doll to Mrs. Lot for her collection?"

"Mrs. Lot? She would faint for joy, I guess. She'd wave her
handkerchief to fan herself, and smile like anything."

"Then if you took your dimes and brought your little brother
Butch that autographed baseball he's always wanted, what would
Butch do?"

"Oh, first he would hug me; then laugh. First thing we know,
he'd be rounding up the other little kids from town, and there
would be a fast game going in no time."

Mother smiled that sly, drowsy smile she uses when she thinks
she's won an argument.

"And would the reaction of these people as they received
your gifts make you feel better?"

"Oh, sure," I agreed. "But I still would have nothing left for
me."

"You would. You would have the happy memories of the things
you have just described to me; memories which no one could

steal from you. Life is just a series of giving; those who give most have pleasant memories, for those trade deeds for them. As long as you have good memories, you have something more precious than diamonds, and you will have learned that it is impossible to give away all you possess."

But as a child, I thought as a child. The meaning of this creed was still a riddle to me in my world of many confusing riddles. Certainly there was an answer someplace; if I could only find it, I could find happiness in this world of people which I could not understand.

In mysteries the solution comes from following clues. Perhaps there were clues around that I could not see. Where to begin? That was a question that answered itself with more questions. Could it be that people were riddles? Were they the little riddles which solved the big ones? Were the little riddles locked arm in arm with big ones? People were hard to solve, I found, because each person was so many people all in one; people, like my jackstones, were always landing with one side up, and then the other side up, until I was never sure which side to expect. The riddle still puzzled me when I was ten, for it was at this age that with a solemn oath in blood — a straight pin's prick of my sucked-clean thumb — I dedicated my life to a career in writing as only a ten-year-old can.

My tenth birthday was made more memorable by a visit from Miss Cosey Walters who had taught school down where Maumee Coal Company had built Tipple Number Three years before I was born. The school is empty with its shutters boarded and its chimney sagging, yet Cosey never lets one forget she taught there. I went to my upstairs bedroom while she visited with Mother in the living room below; here I could lean, unobserved by Mother's censuring eyes, into silent laughter which Cosey's words evoked. My dresser, polished red to match the woodwork which my great-grandfather had cut from oaks on the Homeplace, held a clock by which I timed the length of Cosey's visit, a family joke. Her thin tenor voice seemed to bounce on each step of the winding staircase; she had lumped her one hundred and eighty pounds into the sagging leather chair that had been my great-grandfather's favorite.

"I was just tellin' over at Lots' about how lucky your family was, Bonnie. Both you and Jay named Miller and marryin' up. It be a good thing you weren't related, because everyone knows such inbreeds have idiot offspring," Cosey began.

I picked up my Johnny Appleseed book and idly fanned the tiny, worn pages as I stretched on my stomach across my bed. The sun shining through the triple windows which opened out onto a roof was as yellow as my chintz bedspread.

Cosey caught her breath before her next sentence. "I know that book of hymns and poetry is your little Myra's joy, but she should learn to read other good books. That book *Jakeyville Journal,* the one Helen wrote about our town, sure ain't fit for children here in Genesis County to read. A pity they let a book like *Jakeyville Journal* in our library! This town ain't much with the coal all taken from underneath it, but we still got our decency."

At least seven different maneuvers of Cosey's to snag a husband had ended in failure, but she had swallowed her pride and exercised her maternal instinct on the children of the children who had once been her pupils. That was common knowledge about Cosey which I accepted as everyone else did.

"So I brought your Myra a good book for her birthday. And by the way, Bonnie, did that man ever come back to see her about getting the Johnny Appleseed book for that museum he's plannin'? Sure would be a good thing if she'd give it, but I know how she feels, it bein' in the family for so long."

"I'm sure Myra will appreciate your gift, Cosey," Mother agreed. "But as to Myra's book being given to the museum, it will have to be her decision alone. It's hers. And while, as the collector said when he came here to see it, it would do a great deal of good toward teaching how the words of God were once brought into Indiana, Myra cherishes it for its family attachment."

Fifty-five minutes later Cosey came to the real point of her visit. Mother's sigh, for she had ironing to finish and supper to get before P.T.A. meeting that night, was audible.

"Hate to be a nuisance, but could I bother you for another piece of your Genesis Tree? Too bad the strippers came in to plow up the old burial cemetery on the Homeplace, but yours is the last tree like it, and I believe in keepin' the old community relics alive.

I could hear Cosey following Mother out through the dark hall to the dining room with its heavy oak furniture with lion's head legs. When they passed the curved-glass china closet with its delicately painted, fragile cups swaying from metal hooks, the precious, hoarded, frangible china dishes chattered to protest Cosey's weighty momentum. Cosey paused before the cabinet to chew her hairy upper lip in silent envy.

"The Genesis Tree is still quite young," Mother said. "The side garden gives it the best protection. I'm sure it will grow and live for many years. It has a good start now. I'll get a knife and a paper to wrap the cutting in."

The rectangular-shaped garden, bordered by a white fence along the road, stretched beyond the stone winterhouse. Inside the winterhouse, dark and damp, were winter-stored the orchard's red apples, the brown, tight-skinned potatoes, the swelling green cabbage heads, the kraut keg, and the mangoes in their vinegar barrel. Swung overhead in net bags were onions and popcorn clustered in orange ear-bouquets. That particular summer the garden border of tulips extended past the rose-trellised summerhouse where ramblers leapt, spring-green, to rival the heady purple lilacs and the squat snowball bushes. At ten, I actually believed that the original Eden, where the Tree of Knowledge first grew, must have rated as second to Indiana in the spring. Cosey followed Mother up the brick path. Their passing disturbed the hummingbirds as they visited the sweet honeysuckle.

Perhaps when my own grandmother was a girl she had watched the garden below her, and from these same triple windows, as I now watched Mother and Cosey in the garden below me. Propped up on my elbows, I listened as the old house magnified the sound of their voices. Cosey's dark, bunned hair was covered by her limp-brimmed hat which waved up and down as she walked; that wasn't all that moved when Cosey walked. Seeing her, I wanted Mother, then turning twenty-nine, never to let herself get so broad. I was proud of Mother's still-young slenderness when I compared them. It seemed that sloppier women, those who wore print housedresses, pin curls, and anklets as a universal uniform on the street, were the bearers of the stamp of marriage. I hated their weary stoop and fat, unconfined lumps.

I could hear Cosey's confidences. "I didn't want to say anything your little Myra could overhear." They walked on. "Little pitcher, big ears and all that. But didn't that *Jakeyville Journal* book Helen wrote just describe some of the folks around here to a T?"

"Not quite," Mother discouraged as she stopped to snip off a rambler trailer in passing. She popped her pricked finger into her mouth. "The people in Helen's book all lived in other times, times like those of the Civil War. Now all are in their graves, forgotten. But, yes, some of the people in those books were taken from real life. I often heard my grandmother Cynthy Miller tell how her father returned to fight for the South, while her older brothers joined up with the North when they were fourteen. Theirs was just one of the families divided by their loyalty and the unrest of those times."

"Exactly what I mean," Cosey agreed. "I tell you we're all in the same boat. Some of our people were right in that *Jakeyville Journal* book. Especially in those community gatherings they held. George Dillen Hawroth used to say, when people gathered round to hear those yarns he spun about Genesis County, that all his story characters were fictitious, but we know better. Some's plain as day, real life."

"Yet storytellers of myths are not supposed to use real people. They can be sued." Mother pinned back a bit of hair that a briar had mussed. "Cousin George spent his life, even though he could have made a good living as a geologist, running down all the folklore in Indiana. He collected the myths as a hobby, that's all. His characters weren't all real people."

"Not supposed to use real characters, but they do. People can't help being people . . ."

"I guess you're right, Cosey. That's how God made us, so it must be good in His sight."

"Could be it's sort of a coincidence. Now you take that preacher out of *Jakeyville Journal.* Seems history's just repeated itself."

They rounded the summerhouse on the circular path and passed the tallest lilac tree. The move brought them closer to the house.

"That preacher in the book of Helen's," Cosey continued after catching her breath. "He's almost a dead ringer for that Preacher Brother Gorby. Did you hear about him?"

When Mother shook her head, Cosey beamed as though her name had just been called in a raffle. "Well he's that new young evangelist who conducted that meetin' over on Coon Dog Creek several weeks back. He was doin' real well, too. Them sisters from Cherubim Township was a-flockin' up to the Mourner's Bench, awhoopin' and ahollerin' to who tied the cow up. In his heavenly joy, and I admit he was a purty man — seen him myself with that shiny black hair, and them long white hands of his — who danced around that altar to that fast music with the best of 'em. Then, just when the Lord was a really sendin' him convictions, he up and ran off with the piano player. Just like that!" She snapped plump, ruby-ringed fingers.

"Who was the piano player?" Mother stopped before the Genesis Tree to put on her garden gloves.

Cosey took a deep breath, took her handkerchief from its hiding place in a deep, dividing line, faced Mother squarely, and tilted her head to squint into the sun. "Well, it was Rosie-Addie Wakefield, ol' Stubby Wakefield's daughter. They live out in the company-block shacks. Rosie-Addie's mother died in childbirth after that mess Stubby got into. She was a Wilson — good people — remember? Rosie-Addie can't be more'n sixteen. Poor young un' never had much of a chance, anyhow. Her pa, Stubby, is the one that beat that mule to death in the mine back in '29 or '30, remember? Stubby had the drinkin' streak born in him from the Burchel side of the house. Can't help it, they say."

"Poor Rosie-Addie child," Mother sighed. "Stubby drinks his mine check up every payday. Even flickers ahead. Rosie-Addie probably had it so tough at home, she felt getting away — any

way — would be better than living in that awful shack all her life."
She tested the shears, scissoring them open and closed. "Was this
Brother Gorby, the preacher — "

"Married?" Cosey interrupted like thrusting a tray forward to
catch the gravy, at this juicy point, while roasting the young minister on Scandal's Spit. " 'Course he was. Or I guess he was. Preachers
always are and . . . "

Mother bent toward the Genesis Tree, then just a skeleton bush
only five feet high. "Too bad for the girl. I wish there had been
something I could have done for her, something I could have
given her. It's so hard to help the miners' children, though, for the
code is so strong in them." She sighed her regret. "I guess, Cosey,
that it's the times that change here, not the people. People will be
people. Now let's see." Mother counted on the branch she had
selected. "One, two, three nodes. Cutting it here should give you
enough to start you a Genesis Tree."

Cosey restrained herself for a polite moment. Greed crowded
her face like the puffiness above her black tight-laced oxfords.
"Make it a whole branch, Bonnie. I want to be sure this time it'll
live. I'd love to get one started, 'specially after the ones you gave
Bella Tennis and Mary Goss Miller died."

Mother presented the whole branch. Cosey, embarrassed that her
desire to possess something more than Bella or Mary had was
showing her to be a pig, flushed. "That doesn't leave much of a
tree for you'ins, does it?"

"Grandma Miller used to say that the more starts of a plant you
gave away, the more the good Lord would make yours grow. Glad
to oblige." Then came Mother's happiness creed: *"One can never
give away all one possesses!"*

The Genesis Tree, called by some the "Raintree," was imported
to Indiana years ago. Interest in it flourished when George Dillen
Hawroth began to collect and to tell the stories of the Indian myths
connected with the county. He said that he thought the Tree of
Knowledge, spoken of in the Bible, might be the Genesis Tree, and
that if he could trace its origin he might help discover the solution
to the riddle of Life itself, although he laughed when he said it to

let everyone know he wasn't serious. The people laughed with him.

I wondered then why people laughed when they mentioned their thoughts like that. Did it really embarrass them when their thoughts were not what thoughts are supposed to be? Or were they afraid of being laughed at for thinking about things they could not understand? Did they feel as guilty as I did when I asked if Santa Claus were real and the grownups laughed at me?

So the people had laughed right along with George, I guess, until that streak of lightning, during a freak summer storm, killed him out in Eden Swamp, near Shakamak, one day.

When the news got around that Mother had brought the last Genesis Tree to our garden, Cosey wasn't the only greedy person who wished to get a start from the tree. The curious ones followed as the argument over whether or not it was the Tree of Life for certain grew from the gossip people created around the "God sent" manner in which George died. Was it really the flaming sword God set up that day in the Garden of Eden that killed him? The desire for *possession* of the tree as a momento was the fire gleaming in the eyes of those who came begging for a "start." It was almost impossible to grow a tree from its seed.

The Genesis Tree seekers drove up in shiny cars to park along the road. The would-be possessors would lean against the white fence. While one chewed on a green stem, the plan of approach would be mapped. After a few minutes the delegate, the most venturesome of the group, would come up to the walk that began at the iron gate, pause at our porch, and say, "Is this the old Miller place where the real Genesis Tree grows?"

From the dark regions of our house Mother would come, her wide white teeth gleaming in her patient smile, so traditional a part of Indiana's hospitality. "Yes. That's what my grandfather, Pete Miller, called it over on the Homeplace."

"Was he the Pete Miller they called the 'Fiddlin' Man'? Fiddled at all the square dances around here, didn't he? Often heard my grandfather speak of him."

"The same, I guess."

"And he taught school, all seven grades in one room, didn't he?

Had that farm near Shakamak before they took part of it to make the park? George Dillen Hawroth used to tell about the Shakamak often as his boyhood playground."

They would speak with Mother of the bygone virgin days when the Genesis Tree grew like a huge umbrella in the dark woods by the Shakamak, its yellow fronds dripping from the ends of the branches to look like yellow rain or a great sheltering yellow cape.

After following Mother into our garden the seeking strangers would stand beside her small tree to finger its narrow leaf and its yellow hanging flower cluster. Before the strangers left, after all their "Ohs!" and "Ahs!" and "I would just love to have's," they would get a start from the Genesis Tree.

While watching from my upstairs bedroom window, my anger would ball up inside me like a clenched fist. The Genesis Tree was Mother's, not theirs! Oh, why couldn't they see that with each branch greedily stripped they took a piece of Mother's life? The Genesis Tree tied our family together, the symbol of living. Love must be nourished to exist; sin begins only when love is dead; to hold anything back — not to give — is sin itself. Yet Mother loved, with childlike, selfish tenderness, each yellow flower, each leaf . . . as if each were a part of her, somehow. True to her creed, she could never refuse those who asked.

If the secret of life ever becomes the property of man, it will have something to do with love, I know. Love of family, love of the land, love of creation, love of God and as many loves as there are people on the earth. Again and again I asked myself: Why do my people love the Genesis Tree so much? Does it hold the answer to the riddle: *what creature is it that in the morning of its life . . . ?* Is it a symbol of something I cannot understand now or ever? They say that all things in life or love must have a beginning. But where?

As far back as I can remember it seemed that living was a series of giving.

That summer evening when I was eleven was one of those times. The four of us were sitting around the supper table. Fall crispness in the air outside made Daylight shiver as Darkness pushed her aside so that Night could have a place to look in at us through the bay window. We were laughing when we heard a timid knock at our back door. Butch didn't stop eating, but I did.

Mother pushed back her chair and rose from the table just as Mrs. Cain, a neighbor, popped her head inside the kitchen. Mrs. Cain quickly withdrew her gray-streaked head as an indication that she wished to speak to Mother in the privacy of our back porch.

Their whispers weren't audible to my listening ears.

Moments later Mother dashed into the kitchen, turned off the burner under the coffee, and said, "I'm running over to the Cains' for a minute."

"What's the matter now?" Butch paused long enough to ask.

"Nothing at all," she replied. "Be right back." She picked up the coffeepot in one hand, an apple pie from the cooling rack with the other.

"Hey, I wanted that," Butch protested, his mouth full.

"Finish on something else. There's — " Mother's words were cut short as the door slammed behind her.

"Maybe they're starving to death over there, so I guess she'd rather starve us." Butch began to seek sympathy for the loss of pie.

"I don't think so," Dad said. "You'll live."

"Then what's going on over at Cains'?" I asked. "There's always an uproar in that Cain family. Quarrel all the time. Drinking, too. Patty told me that her father guessed Bill Cain would turn into pickle preserves he's been pickled so often, and that those boys of his are going to be just like him. Patty said that her mother said that that house of theirs smelled just like a brewery, and that if she had anything to do with it, she'd — "

"Slow down, Myra," Dad laughed. "You kids hear too much gossip for your years. Maybe someone is sick over there and needs help. So who do they come for? Your mother. As simple as that."

"And away she goes," said Butch. "Never caring whether I have anything to eat or not. It's just like her to grab up food without a minute's explanation."

"You look hungry," I teased, and passed him the crusts of bread I would not eat.

We finished our meal, and when Mother still didn't return I took her sweater down from a hook in the pantry. Wouldn't it seem thoughtful of me to take the sweater to Mother at Cains' house so that she would have it when she came back in the cold? That way I could find out what was going on over there.

That night was so dark that the stars were too ashamed to twinkle as I cut through a vacant lot to make my trip shorter. Dry weeds scratched my legs with their swishing until my feet found a narrow path which I followed, guided by the lights from the windows of the Cains' house which looked foreboding at the end of the lane.

There were some loose boards on the sagging back porch. I felt for them, one foot cautiously in front of the other, until my hands found the latch of the paint-peeling door.

Timidly, but without knocking, I peeked in at the kitchen. The large room had grease-yellowed walls which made the plaster lumps, hand patched, look more pronounced in the artificial light. The gray-patterned linoleum was spattered in places with blood. A round table, burdened with disarrayed dishes, had been pushed into a corner already blocked by an upright cabinet of dark wood. Mrs. Cain, slumped and dejected, sat on a chair, in her hand a half-empty cup of coffee — ours. One of the Cain boys, the taller, Cam, was washing blood from his face and hands at the sink in the corner where a pitcher pump was making a sucking noise. Cam must have been all of nineteen, but I have never seen a man cry as he was crying then.

"Don't walk in that blood, Myra," Mother cautioned as I stood with my mouth hanging open. "I'll clean it up when I'm finished in here."

I strained my eyes to seek Mother in the dimly lit dining room beyond the kitchen. She was down on her knees beside a couch and on it was stretched, on his stomach, the younger brother, Abe, while she bathed a small wound in his shoulder with the contents of a basin on the floor beside her. Mr. Cain was seated at the dining-room table and looked as if he hadn't shaved in a month of Sundays.

"Oh, what did I ever do so God would punish me like this?"
Mr. Cain chanted over and over as if he expected an answer from
the sleazy curtains and frayed blind at the window across the room.
"Never thought one of my sons woulda took up arms and kilt the
other."

"Abe's not dead, Bill," Mother said crisply. "Just a flesh wound."
I could not seem to move from the spot until I heard Mother say,
"Myra, run on home and call Dr. Lillie, will you?"

This roused Mrs. Cain. "Oh, you're not going to have to call a
doctor, are you?" she begged.

"I'm afraid we'll have to," Mother explained. "It's the law,
but I'm sure we can work out the bill if that's the trouble."

Mrs. Cain hesitated while swishing the coffee around in her
cup. "Not all of it, anyways. It's the people at my church. At
church . . . well, at church I wouldn't want 'em to hear about —
oh, well, Pa makes a little drinkin' beer down in the cellar. You
know what'd happen if the saints down at the church heard about
it. You know." She shook her head mournfully and tried in vain
to pin straying hair into the knot at the nape of her neck. "Sure
as a doctor's called — "

"Yes," Mother agreed as she brought the shallow gray pan with
its red, liquid contents to empty into the sink, already red-spattered
from Cam's use of it. "There is your standing at church to think of.
But Myra, you just go right on to call the doctor and I'll think of
something while he's coming. And Myra," she cautioned as she
began to wipe up blood spots from the linoleum, "not a word to
anyone, understand? Come back as soon as you can. Okay?"

My heart pounded as I flew home with my message.

"What's your hurry?" Dad called down from upstairs as I
phoned.

"One of the Cains is hurt. Mother wanted a doctor." I hurried
out of the door before Dad could ask more. I didn't want to miss
any of the excitement.

After the doctor had paid his visit, Mother and I walked home
together. She carried the coffeepot and we shared her sweater.
"But this fracas at the Cains' didn't happen just the way Mrs. Cain

told the doctor, did it? It wasn't an accident while cleaning a gun, was it?"

Mother waited a while before replying. "Well, it *was* an accident, in a way. The Cains are an almost destitute family, one I never knew too well. Bill, the father, drank up his money when he mined; then he started making his own drink in the cellar. Jakeyville's people have had to look after the family for years. The boys were never given a chance. Always played hooky from school. Haven't turned out too well, I'm afraid."

"Then that's what the fight was about. Over drinking. Is that why Cam shot Abe?"

"Yes, I guess so."

"Then why didn't you have the doctor call the police to arrest Cam? That's what's right."

"Is it, Myra?" Mother asked after a while. "Let's say it's like buying a new dress. To be sure it's worth the money you have to examine the seams and hem. People decide by things like that, too. If the police had been called and Abe had pressed charges, Cam would have been jailed. Cains had no money for defense lawyers, not even enough for the doctor, but I'll pay him. Soon those boys will be drafted. Maybe they'll learn a new, useful sort of existence. It was Effie I was thinking of. The only place she has in life is in her church, and I'm afraid her church wouldn't be too tolerant of one of its 'sisters' with beer in her cellar. She's kept the secret from the other 'saints' so far; an investigation would have revealed her secret shame. The church would no longer be her one haven from the stormy sort of life she has at home or will have when her boys are gone."

We had reached the end of their lane and crossed the gravel road.

"So you just stood there while she told the doctor that lie. Didn't the doctor know better?"

"Probably. He had to take her word, so that protects him. But I think the whole Cain family learned a lesson, a sobering-up lesson. Maybe it's God's way of making them stop and think, perhaps change."

"Why did you take the pie and coffee when you left? How did you know what kind of trouble?"

"I didn't, but knowing the situation, I guessed. Most of our trouble can be solved when we're calmer. Time out for eating calms us all. And it worked for Effie Cain, didn't it?"

"It helped her, yes. But what's she ever done for you?"

Mother's laugh confused me further. "Oh, I don't know. Just always been here in Genesis County, I guess. Maybe it's because she lets me do things for her, help her out when she's in trouble like tonight. It's making me feel needed that I owe her for."

"And what about the doctor's bill? Money just given away."

"That again? You know it's impossible to give away all I possess. I have you and Butch and your dad and all the people in Genesis County to love. Who needs more?"

I couldn't understand Mother's reasoning except that it made me feel good to be out walking with her this way, to share her confidences, and to come back to my own home after visiting the Cains.

"I can't understand about Effie Cain's church. Isn't it to be a refuge? Would they have thrown her out, really?" I begged.

"Some churches have strong rules about things, not Christian rules like the ones God made and meant us to keep — like charity for all."

"And the Cains are poor, Mother? So poor that other churches send them baskets so they'll have something to eat?"

We had reached our back yard. " 'Fraid so."

"Then where do they get money to make beer?"

Mother laughed again as she paddled me up the porch steps. "All I know is that you're much too nosy for a child your age."

The riddle of the haves and have-nots was mine to solve alone. All these things for which I must search became a symbol of the unsolved riddle. And as I decided the riddle might be easier to solve if I could get all of the pieces together, I began to describe the characters around me in writing.

For three long years I continued to write. From this I learned that I was neither a genius nor a very good detective. Thousands of words peeked out above my typewriter ribbon. Rejected, all of them, but thrill came from the letters which editors were kind enough to write when they sent my brain-chickens home to roost.

Again, when I was fourteen, the four of us sat around the supper table in the kitchen; again the Genesis Tree entered our conversation.

Mother passed the meat platter to Dad. "I went over to Shakamak Park today. Stole an afternoon off."

"Three guesses why? To get woods dirt for the Genesis Tree, I suppose." Dad grinned. "Honestly, Bonnie, the way you baby that young tree ever since bringing it over here from the Homeplace. Been like one of the family, almost." His pride in Mother's tree hid between his teasing syllables.

"Baby? That tree gets more attention than I do," Butch argued as he liberally jellied his butter-bread. His lips never missed a beat of the mouthful-chewing rhythm. His burr-clipped head was bent to the pleasant task of wolfing down his food. "You tell us that it's wrong to steal anything but second base, yet you dig on state property just to get dirt for that oversized fern of yours. It's a privileged character round here. And just a skinny, sick-looking tree, too!"

"It wasn't always skinny," I defended, feeling my color rise to rival my freckles. "Left alone it would grow into a huge, mushroomed tree that would drip to the earth in yellow rain. But it needs shade, the solitude of a place it once knew naturally, and not all these morbid, sensation-hungry people tearing it up for pieces. Don't they realize it's the very last one?"

"That's why they want it, Myra," Dad said. "The scarcer, the dearer — the way it is with all such old things."

"It's like antiques," Mother explained. "For a long time no one truly appreciated the Genesis Tree. Now Indiana and the world are becoming more legend conscious. It's only natural that people wish to own something of their native soil. It's a form of riches."

"And what killed them out in the first place? Wasn't it the dollar-hungry who flocked to Indiana? Farmers first, yes. Then came the strippers' shovels to get the coal underneath the topsoil. They leave behind the ugly shale-mud pits that yawn as if to say, There's nothing here; not of beauty, not of anything! Most of our young people move away. The old-timers stay on to reminisce until they die. All these people . . . being people!'"

"It's the land that makes the people, Myra," Mother reminded. "And the people must return to make the land. That's the law in life, in love, in everything you do. No one deserts the land from which he sprang, not in his heart at least."

I didn't like them to preach, but would have forgiven them.

"Methinks," Dad said while winking the way he does when he feels he is cleverly talking over our heads, "that our book-struck daughter, the one with two heads and little filling except printer's ink, who yearns to be T. S. Eliot plus Kilgallen, has been sneaking around reading *Jakeyville Journal.*"

"Wasn't sneaking. It's in Jakeyville's Library." My eyes implored Mother to come to my defense. She did.

"Well, Myra wants to become a writer. Writers must first be readers. Helen's *Journal* is no worse than Joyce's *Portrait* you gave her for Christmas, some of Hemingway's, and some of that Jones boy's who wrote a best seller within a stone's throw. Helen's book told about people like us; that's why we resent it. It's part of growing up. Myra will have to learn to cut away the bad from the good, much as she will have to learn to cut away the bad in herself, and others, from the good."

"But this matter of sex, Bonnie." Dad coughed, embarrassed.

"Is it forbidden fruit? There's no soft pedal on this generation as far as reading matter goes. You'll have to admit that novelists are being realistic. Exaggerating, yes. But honest."

"Heard a joke today at the diamond," Butch offered as he speared his third pork chop. "Seems a writer was gathering facts for a modern novel over here on the campus. He asked a coed if she had read *Jakeyville Journal,* and she said — "

I lifted my iced-tea glass to drink, and watched Dad's face through the bottom of the glass, a masculine face, fair, slender, and finished handsomely with a dimple in the chin.

"Now that will bury such talk at the table, Butch." He laughed into Mother's eyes. "What creature is it that in the morning of its life . . . ?"

"Exactly," she continued. "The *Indianapolis Views* called the

Journal a 'documentary list of southern Indiana.' If it's in the *Views* — "

"If it's in the *Views,* it's because Editor Edward Pullman wants it there for a Republican fact!" Dad added sugar to his tea and stirred the spoon around vigorously. As a Democrat, one of the few in Indiana, he resented the Republican-controlled press. "Even then the *Views* is a *good* paper — a fact which having a large circulation doesn't prove."

"You carried it and so did I," Butch added. "Betcha my boy doesn't carry it. By that time each house will have its own wire service, wait and see. I can just see that long line of writers out of work. Poor Myra will be one. What a tragedy to see her have to go to work at last. That'll teach her not to be so snoopy. That'll teach her not to be so selfish, too. Just 'cause she's got that Johnny Appleseed book of hers, she won't lend it or let anyone buy it. Not able to get a job, Myra'll come over to my house begging — "

"And when I do, I'll send you a telegram first. That way, if you can get any of your friends to read to you, you'll be the first to know. And as for my book, Cousin George meant for me to have it. It's family and I'll not have strangers gawking at it in a case! Mother, if you don't make Butch be still, I'll murder that worm — "

"Nothing like the brotherly love in this house," Dad laughed.

"If he lives to graduate from grade school, it'll surprise me."

"Butch will. Wait and see. I had my troubles when I carried the *Views,* too. Remember back when we caught Cosey Walters planning that rendevouz over in Eden Swamp with Superintendent Sappington?" Dad asked Mother. "He told us that he was on his way across to take Cosey a copy of the *Views,* with Lindbergh's speech in it, to use in her class. As *Views* carriers, we couldn't look at a copy after that without thinking of 'The Spirit of St. Louis'; after that it was Sappington's name from then on. Behind his back, of course. The policy of the *Views* hasn't changed much since then. Times have changed, not the people."

Dad's laughter about Cosey was not unkind. Tolerant is a better word. Yet I wondered how and why people could laugh about promiscuity when the Bible was so definite about it being a sin.

Stealing was also a sin, yet Mother stole the woods dirt from Shakamak without wincing. Why did older people make the rules and then be tolerant of those who broke them? No, I promised myself, I could never learn to be that tolerant. This promise was to bring my greatest heartbreak.

❋

It was much later on, in my sixteenth summer, that we felt, rather than noticed, the rapid change for the worse in Mother's health. We became as the quail and possum: "Let's be quiet, maybe the hound will go away!"

When our evening meal was finished one night I stood up to wiggle my bare toes back into damp moccasins and to pull my damp shorts away from my hips.

"You were writing in the woods again today, Myra!" Mother teased. "Perched alone on that moss-covered Moses rock up a creek. Someday a snake or a bear will get you."

"That creek's a lake, and there are people worse than bears. Wolves." I whistled.

"That's what I dig," she explained as she stacked glasses. "You're getting too grown up. Boys notice, I take it." She laughed at my crushes on boys, as interested as any of my friends.

"Watch your language, madam." I smiled down at the salt and pepper shakers in my hand. "The woods aren't as desirable as Hemingway's yacht, over at 'The Last Resort,' or up where Indiana's Thoreau plays Dickens beside his lake, but they're the best place I've found to write in my notebook. Cool and dark. Who can say there is a better place than in the woods which are filled with mood words?

"At times I seem to hear Miami Indians still filing down the paths, the Quakers going to meeting, young lovers hunting privacy while trees whisper of their passions, and the complaining creek arguing politics with all the rolling pebbles that gather no moss, scolding them."

I helped scrape the dishes while doing mambo steps to the disc jockey's platters, spun from the little ivory radio above the sink. Mother washed and I dried the dishes.

While carrying the heavy stack of clean dishes to the cabinet, I wondered why the clean, sterile heat arising from them gave me satisfaction. Was it the well-being of a tiresome task finished? Or was it because doing dishes is such a thankless chore, yet so unending, to be done again and again, that it made me feel important and necessary? Was part of the riddle a feeling that you are part of a pattern?

Mother went out into the garden which was her pride. Soon voices, floating in, interrupted my thoughts. Looking through the bay window, as three generations of my father's family had done before me, I saw a car stop by our fence. Soon Mother, even though her tiredness grew more evident day by day, would answer the same questions asked by our uninvited visitors. Didn't they know she had been up all last night with ol' Mrs. Laban, a neighbor dying of cancer? The acts of these visitors puzzled me. Why did people wait until something became a rarity before they wanted it? Like antiques, for instance. And a fatal illness on its last cell. Just because it was the last Genesis Tree, now they were eager to get a start. Was that why people called upon the dying, or visited the dead, instead of coming to call when their visit might have been mutually enjoyed? I would hate to think that people looked upon the bier just to gloat and say: "Look, I have life! What do you know that I don't? Have you discovered a secret in death?"

I climbed the steps leading up to my room. The prayer pasted above my desk gave little comfort as my worry about Mother's health increased. In my heart, I associated her generosity in parting with her beloved Genesis Tree, piece by piece, with her decline.

The prayer read: Give me the courage to change the things I can, to accept those I cannot, and the knowledge to know the difference.

How could it be true — this belief of Mother's — I asked myself. *It's impossible to give away all you possess.* Wasn't she giving away the thing she loved so selfishly? What was she trying to prove by driving herself when she was ill? What would she have when all of the Genesis Tree was gone? . . .

I felt somehow that I was being left out of her life. I was jealous that I could not be first. As I often did when the puzzle got too complicated, I shut out the voices of the scavengers in the garden below my triple windows by stretching out on my stomach across my bed. I flipped the pages of my soiled, worn half diary, half notebook to . . .

REJOIN THE SEARCH

Had I been just seven when I had gone with Mother on her last visit to the Homeplace? The state had built a road dividing the original Miller farm; the larger part was incorporated by Indiana into Shakamak Park. The years of growth had barricaded the park with the density of giant pines and cedars. On the other side of the road, the remaining part of my great-grandfather's Homeplace was deserted. Here all of my mother's family had grown up to live, to laugh, and to sleep in the burial plot on the hill in back of the farm. The road which once lead to this plot had long ago been overgrown. Thick, verdant weeds and wildflowers searched for subsistence around the roots of the pines where the old frame house had once stood. Two giant firs stood sentry there where the broad door had often opened.

Morgan's men once set fire to the Homeplace when they raided this far north during the war. My Great-grandfather Miller, the Fiddlin' Man, rebuilt the Homeplace after that. His wife left family records which told how she and her brothers had taken the cow, the horses, and the sow — carrying her litter of new pigs in a basket — deep into the woods so that raiders would not carry them off as they did the chickens and geese. "And even worse things that could happen to little girls," her mother had warned. Their garden had been looted of young potatoes and beans; the rest was burned in the meaningless urge to destroy, the urge that hides deep in the waters of each man's heart, and surfaces with the excuse of war.

Parts of the chimneys at each end of the house were still standing; defying even in their uselessness the giant stripper's shovels
that were coming to rob the land of the poorer grades of coal, that
which the deep mines hadn't taken. The Miller family had sold
the Homeplace land, bit by bit. Poverty, failure of crops in the poor
clay soil that was left, and need had made them sell out to the
Maumee Company. The money they used only to settle the debts
they had inherited with the land, but more debts accumulated with
the years.

Mother and I stood that day before the old, tottering chimney
that spilled its handmade brick. I bent over to take into my child's
hands the cool brick and held the red fragment there under the
shade of the hovering oak tree, held it because I felt I must feel
things with my hands in order to understand them. The brick was
crumbling, as all of us will someday crumble.

"It is old, Mother?" I asked. "And it is dirty."

"Old, yes." I looked up to see her eyes were wet. "But not
dirty. Nothing in this land is dirty."

"Even though it makes my hand dirty?" I rubbed my palms on
my shorts.

"There is *dirt* that rubs off the hands; this dirt is washed back
eventually to the earth. Real *dirt* is the corruption that clings to
the heart and mind — the smut that gossip harbors. That's the
kind that cannot be washed away like this kind of dirt. *That evil
dirt* returns to the earth only when the evil generations forget the
acts of their dead, forget to hate, and their reason for hating . . . "

I couldn't understand her meaning then, just like all the many
other things about life I could not understand. When she took
the spade from the trunk of the car, she didn't stop crying; hers
was not a wild, angry crying, but a faint moan like the wind in the
chimney of my bedroom at night when all but thought is quiet.

I followed Mother up the hill, the sun warm on the backs of my
legs as we climbed. She stopped before the Genesis Tree, the last
of its kind in the county. I watched in silence at the edge of the
fenced-in graveyard.

With the reluctant spade, she gently turned down the covers

of the tender young tree's bed. Then, kneeling reverently, as if God dwelt within the branches of the Genesis Tree to direct her searching fingers, she rocked the root threads that defended themselves from being rent from the mother-earth. Whisper-groaning, with the sigh of a surrendering lover, the tree shuddered free. The roots begged, in moist droplet-clods, to take this bit of Homeplace soil with them to the new home in the lilac-and-honeysuckle garden beside our house. Lifted to the spread newspaper, the rooted tree was cloud-wrapped by Mother's hands, caressing in her love for her family's past proud history that the Genesis Tree symbolized with its memories.

"Is it truly the last Genesis Tree, Mother," I asked because I could offer no other solace for her wet-face tears.

"The last, Myra, honey. And always — " She stopped to brush her tears away on the back of her hand, and never finished her sentence. I followed her in silence, like a hound at her heels, as she placed the tree in our car. Again I followed as she returned once more to the burial plot, crested on the hill behind where the house once stood.

She paused before each ancient headstone, knelt and pulled the weeds away to say a last goodbye. The stripper would soon come to destroy the graveyard. Only one would remain unmoved.

She waited longer in front of that headstone than all the others. "George Dillen Hawroth," I read the words aloud. "Born 1914. Died 1947. What cre-creat-shure is it that in the morning of its life...?"

She said nothing. I almost burst to say something to ease her quiet, choking kind of grief, but I was awkward. "And he was a good man, Mother? The storyteller, the one who always made everyone laugh?" I tried to send my voice into her half closed, remembering eyes.

"Yes, the same clown." When Mother smiled, the corners of her mouth stretched up into the past where I could not follow.

"Then why is it you and Daddy laugh at the tricks George used to play as a boy and in college? Like his stealing Great-grandmother's green apples and blaming her favorite calf. Then, suddenly, you look as sad as when someone pulls the blinds down in my room upstairs, to blot out the sun. Is it because he was a distant cousin to both of you, or how he died?"

"You wouldn't understand, Myra," Mother said after a minute had gentled down the hill in search of its lost shadow. "Someday when you must lose a loved one, someday when you look for truth, then you will understand grief. He loved Genesis County and the tree he found. God called him, I guess, because He loved him as much as the people in our county did. He died so full of life, too young."

Mother bent to press her warm lips against the white headstone. As she stood erect, I saw the strain of last-parting, the final good-bye, stretched taut like a fiddle string across her forehead. Did I imagine it, or did I hear the giant, shading oak tree groan? The willows' weeping? The wild grapes grieving to sigh across the goldenrodded field? The mourning doves' lamenting pierced the reverent silence. All was the dirge as she tore herself away from her ancestors.

Mother took my hand and led me stumbling down the path. Again the sunlight, filtering through the trees, made warm splotches on my skinny legs. Was this the beginning of my search for Truth?, the answer to the mystery that George had tried to solve? Perhaps; for there were things which I felt inside me that day, the questions without answers. "Why death?" was one of them. And, without knowing why, my scrawled diary-notebook was begun that night before I went to sleep to dream of the riddles hidden long ago in Genesis County. Perhaps I would be the one to unravel the riddle: *What creature is it that in the morning of its life . . . ?*

I remembered that day well when, later, I heard grownups talking about those others in the graveyard; how the D.A.R. was having the caskets transferred to a newer place, and that my parents refused to let them move George Dillen Hawroth's body. The others, some lying there for much more than a hundred years, would not care to be plowed around by the stripper's great earth-hungry shovels; for they were already dust. But this one? Maybe he was dust, too, and did not care. Why was George buried in that old, forgotten cemetery in the first place? Was he there with the old-dead because of the legends concerning how he died? What was so strange about his being struck by lightning during the sudden storm that blew up in Miller's Woods that day? Was he buried here because he made everyone laugh with his stories? The legends said that those who died by lightning were picked because God loved them most. If none of these ideas answered the question, it must have been because his friends knew that he would have preferred to be here with his people where tons of Genesis County's earth would cover him more deeply. All was hush-hush in my presence.

If I asked to hear the story of his death repeated, the answer was always the same: "You're too young."

Times most vivid were those when my elders circled together, like cows in a pasture, after church on Sunday. I was even more shy than now, but people drew my interest.

" . . . And isn't it strange how the Millers refuse to let the company move George's body? Would have paid more, too, not to have to circle that graveyard. They sure could have used that money . . . "

When the gossipers noticed that I listened, they paused like the quiet after thunder to say gently, "Poor child, Myra. She never knew him, never heard the stories he told. She's too young to understand."

I understood more than they knew. Our family was a giant hen who gathered each chick under her sheltering feathers. In criticism or envy we were as one — inheritors of the good earth of Genesis County.

"People sought George because he spent so much time gathering the old legends," Dad explained when I begged for an answer to the riddle on the porch one summer evening. "People like to hear the history of themselves. When George died so suddenly they remembered that he had been searching for the Tree of Life. It was natural that they associated his death with the flaming sword mentioned in Genesis. People's romantic notion, much like an old wives' tale."

"Do you think it just coincidence that George loved the book I now have, the one Johnny Appleseed brought into Indiana? People say it was an apple that tempted Eve. And George did find the Genesis Tree when everyone said they all were dead, though. Didn't he take a branch and start one for himself beside the burial plot? Was this because they are so hard to start from seeds?"

"Why don't you ask your mother?" Dad evaded my question as fathers often do.

Mother seemed to evade my questions too, in a different way. Again and again I would pester until she delighted me with stories.

"George's parents died, so he lived with my grandparents, Uncle Pete and Cynthy Miller, over on the Homeplace. Cynthy came into possession of a young apple tree, quite a prize. With great care she raised the tree for five years and eagerly counted each blossom; pies that would melt-in-your-mouth were anticipated.

"My mother, your grandmother, Myra, was expecting your Aunt Ruth at the time. The young apples hung there to tantalize her but she didn't dare take one from the small tree just over the fence near the garden. George waited until my Grandmother Cynthy left to sell the butter she churned to customers in Jakeyville. Then with one long leg in pants always too short, for he grew so fast, George pressed down the fence. We ate the forbidden apples out in the barrel-stave hammock. Eve couldn't have enjoyed her apple more." Memory brought her smile.

"Grandmother Cynthy got home just as George was scolding her favorite calf for breaking down the fence and robbing the tree. George was her favorite, just like her own son, so she made a big show for his benefit. Removing the starched sunbonnet she always wore, she scolded the calf soundly."

When the story was over I would pursue my favorite riddle. "Do you think George ever learned that the Genesis Tree was the one like in the Garden of Eden?"

Mother's sigh was streaked with clinging cobwebs of the past. "Who really knows what George discovered? He wanted knowledge so that he could help people to understand themselves. Perhaps the joy of the searchers was all he discovered for certain. It's enough."

But when I made what must have been a mistake — asked why George had to die "at just the age of my Saviour" — a quiet fell to chase laughter into the Forever Land where Pluto reigns. The quiet was like the mourning dove calling across the plowed field on a sunless morning. No one talked within the family's secret, sheltering walls at our house about how George died; it was only the last mysterious echoes of the whisperers that I heard.

The seeds of wanting to find Truth were planted there; the earth around my own roots was stirring to a strange music, a drummer was beating a rhythm that only I seemed to hear. I had to seek out Truth for myself, to discover what made people tick, think, and act as they did. I had to be a writer. Why? Whether it was to find out facts so that I could condemn the people I thought were bad — for writers have a legitimate excuse for looking — or to find words for their defense, I did not know. It was just that I seemed to have no other choice.

Where was the place to begin? Into my notebook went the descriptions of the people around me. What I have learned as a result of searching has put me, quite uneasily, into the seat of judgment. All is drenched with Indiana sunlight, and has bled lifeblood back into the soil of our beloved county. Have I found an answer to what makes people good and what makes them evil? If I have found the answer to this riddle it will be on my notebook pages. The answer will be found in the philosophy taught by the Fiddlin' Man as he tried to teach the art of living to the boy, George Dillen Hawroth. George's story is on the first page. It begins with . . .

PART TWO

George Dillen Hawroth

"The best excuse for loafin' I know is to say you're lookin' fer somethin' lost. Most folks keep on lookin'. fer lost time," the Fiddlin' Man explained while he sat with the boy under the oak tree, "but if they had used it in the first place, they wouldn't have to search. Now some don't care where lost time went, nohow, but them as does find out sure as late frost hurts the strawberries. Seems ain't nobody knows fer sure what he's searchin' fer if God was to ask him right out. Would you, now?"

GEORGE DILLEN HAWROTH

THAT PARTICULAR SUMMER of George Dillen Hawroth's boyhood was pure Indiana. There were the early mornings, before the sun turned down its fleecy comfort to peep out at the earth, when George took his five-gallon pail to fill with plump berries before breakfast.

As he swung down the lane toward home, he could smell side pork sizzling in Aunt Cynthy's kitchen. He hurried to wash the purple stains from his fingertips at the barnyard well, letting the water splash over into the trough where the cows and horses came up from the barn to be watered; green moss covered the trough on the side away from the sun. Aunt Cynthy, he knew from experience, didn't like to have her biscuits "gettin' cold from wait'n' on him."

His day he invested in the many hours he spent as he followed the team with the plow, the disk, and the harrow. There were horses to be fed, cows to be milked.

Uncle Pete, the fiddler, could never forget his prestige — he had taught "all seven grades in one room, mind you" — and consented only to the task of gathering the eggs into a wicker basket at night. With Aunt Cynthy's help, George carried the night's milk out to the "cooler," an oblong, water-filled, lid-covered depression in the earth into which the brown crock jars were placed. With a long-handled skimmer the cream from the jars of morning's milk was removed to a jar in the corner. Butter was churned three times a week and was sold to Aunt Cynthy's regular customers in Jakeyville, three miles away.

Summer nights were even better. Pete and Cynthy loaded their

Model T with musical instruments to travel, if tires were good enough, to the homes of neighbors. Hoe-downs were the best-loved form of entertainment, shared in turn by the hospitality of the group. To the host's house each family, represented by all members ranging from the toddlers up to the old maid aunts who lived with the family, brought their best sandwiches, pies, and cakes. The host furnished the coffee and the rooms, from which the carpets had been removed and the floors scrubbed, for the square-dancers.

Zeke House, the tall redheaded caller, whose huge hands were as red as his hair and as broad as a melon in August, would greet Uncle Pete as he rattled up into the yard.

"Hurry up, Uncle Pete! Time's awastin'. The organ's awaitin' fer you, Aunt Cynthy, so get that fiddle acallin' the tune. George, boy, did you bring that guitar? Mort's mandolin's already tuned and rarin' to go."

Kerosene lamps shook in their wall holders as the neighbors reveled until midnight and later. When the last tune was squeaked out, the wagons and cars were loaded with sleeping offspring. The hand-holding, shy teen-agers parted reluctantly, and the adults filed past, as Uncle Pete rosined his bow before placing it inside the purple-velvet lined case, to thank him for his music. Was it any wonder that the people of Genesis County welcomed at sight the Fiddlin' Man? The "do-si-do-ers," the callers, wooed the dancers at night. And of those too old to dance, and of those too young to do anything but listen, he entertained out under the shade of the oak trees in his yard on Sunday afternoons. The listeners sat on the ground and he in his chair. Each was fascinated by the tales Uncle Pete spun about the County, its history, and legends which came alive by his homespun philosophy. For those who had never learned to read, the Bible lived in the passages he read and explained. Not once did he miss the opportunity of telling them that it had been his own grandfather, John Miller, who was the first preacher to bring the word of God into the territory from Tennessee, and that it was John who had brought the Genesis Tree into the county then.

George could never forget the nights which were spent at study with the old man. Kerosene lamps sputtered a halo of light around the library table.

"Now that was Plato, take him or leave him," Uncle Pete sighed as he closed the book. "We've finished *East Lynn* and *Barriers Burned Away* this week. I guess the reason I favor *Girl of the Limberlost* is on accounta Porter wrote it. E. V. Debs is a comer, too."

When he noticed that George seemed lost in thought, he stopped. "What's your trouble, son. If you're bound to be one of them geologist fellers, ain't no better place to start than right here in Indiana. It'll be a good life's work, somethin' useful — like teachin' school, fer instance. Did I ever tell you I taught all seven grades in — yes, I guess I did. But whenever I see a boy readin' a Bible like you was out in that hammock this afternoon, I know's somethin's ailin' you."

The boy hesitated, placed his pencil between his teeth, and stretched before answering.

"Maybe you could help, but I doubt it. Remember back when we studied the myths about Jupiter, Juno, and those? They were okay as stories, but a professor from the university talked at school today; he said, right in front of everybody, that some people still believed in those myths. People worshiped gods like Buddha — not ours. The teacher got angry. So did I. How can things like this be? What's God going to do to punish those unbelieving people?"

The old man placed his pipe on a glass dish at the edge of the table. Silently he leaned forward, elbows on his knees. "I knew someday you'd ask that, boy. Knew it soon's you brought that last Genesis Tree from the woods to plant out here by the burial plot. The happiest people on this earth are the ones who know enough not to ask about God's judgment, but knowledge is the crossbar of a man's cross. Legends say that your Genesis Tree might well be the Tree of Life from the Bible. Makes people dread what knowledge might cost them. Are you willin' to pay a price you might regret?"

"My Genesis Tree is almost like part of me," George defended. "But what's my tree got to do with it?"

"You know your Bible good as I do. In Genesis it tells: *And the Lord God commanded the man, saying, Of every tree of the garden thou mayest freely eat: But of the tree of knowledge of good and evil, thou shalt not eat of it: for in the day that thou eatest thereof thou shalt surely die.*

"And later, after Adam's sin, God said again: *Behold, the man is become as one of us, to know good and evil: and now, lest he put forth his hand, and take also of the tree of life, and eat, and live for ever . . ."*

"Yes," the boy replied softly. "It's plain God doesn't want man to know the secret of Life, but He didn't care for us to learn what it is to have to die, did He? And why doesn't He kill off all these other religions not like ours? All I ask is knowledge, to know."

"To ask for knowledge is not sinful. With it a man can become a king; it is doubting that makes him a pauper. The secret of Life is one God means to keep secret from man; it is not good to question. These other religions which bother you are much like the principles of ours if you boil 'em down. I can't explain why God permits them to operate no more than David or Solomon could explain away Baal's worship by heathen wives. Take this James Joyce, best Irish writer they locked the doors on, who tried to find the answer to man's relationship to his Heavenly Father and got lost in the searching. I'm no man to answer you, George, for you have a seekin' mind and will not find rest for it until you know the truth. Remember this: when a man begins to doubt, he robs the coffers of his mind and heart. Empty, a man cannot find peace. For, like Thomas, he aches to place his searching fingers to the nailprints in His hand. He will walk as a blind man in the dark, knowing that sooner or later he'll stumble. He will be drivin' Apollo's chariot too near the sun."

The silence between them was scratched by the wall clock's ticking. The old man rocked in his chair, his glasses folded into his hand. "And so, George? . . ."

"After I read the story of creation, I went out to the Genesis Tree by the graveyard this afternoon to think it over. I looked at the epitaphs on the gravestones of my people. They were all people of God. Why do they die? Where are they now? What purpose did they have in living? Once life was everything to them, but life goes on without them there where the Tree of Life and Truth flourishes. Why, I don't know."

George leaned back in his straight chair. He clasped his intertwined fingers across his young chest and closed his eyes. There was a hidden teardrop in each tear-moist word he could not cry. "God exists, I know just as surely as I know that the Garden of Eden might well have been right here in Indiana. But He created the Kaiser, didn't he? Let us have war? And why did He make Seth Ham black, Enos Japeth yellow, and me white? Why do people hate each other, kill for greed? And lust? Why Cosey that day with Superintendent Sappington — and him married?. . .

"We know only that our God is all wise," the old man replied in a grave voice from a faraway place. "Religion is somethin' between a man and his God, something he must work out alone. Only atheists I ever knew spent most of their time tearin' God down, so it proves if they are so sure they're right, why don't they just shut up? But they're not, not at all sure. I figure that's the reason God planned it so one man can't know what another one's thinkin'. Adam didn't know what Eve was aplannin' or the whole world might have been different."

"That's another *why*. Why Adam? Why Eve? I've got to know, got to!" The anger of the boy's frustration filled the room like the smell of newmown hay at cutting time.

"And do you expect to find it here?"

"Why not? God said that if one took of the Tree of Life, one might live forever."

"And didn't it also say there in Genesis that He would place a flaming sword, which turned in every direction, which would slay everyone who came to seek the Tree of Life?"

"Yes, I guess He did. But maybe He didn't mean me. I want to find Truth for a different reason — not to exploit it; maybe for the good it could do, help others, you know. That reason."

The old man chuckled to help bring them back from the Garden of Eden to Indiana. "Your argument reminds me of what Stubby

Wakefield told one night when he was drinkin'. Told it about Cosey Walters. Said she never missed a sermon and told the preacher why. 'It sure delights me, Brother, to watch the faces of them that needs your sermons. You can just tell that they know you're atalkin' about them.' Is that how you'll defend your search for the Tree of Life, boy?"

George laughed and stretched his legs; the room had returned to the parlor that it was in the beginning. "You can always find a joke — or make one up like those myths you tell. But you've never been troubled by things like this in your day. You always knew about God, were always sure."

"The doubt of Thomas and the mark of Cain is on all of us, boy. We're as guilty as sin. Me too. There's a story out of my boyhood I don't tell others. You need it."

Uncle Pete cleaned his glasses on a bandanna handkerchief before placing them on his high-bridged nose.

"Why do you put on your glasses to tell a story?" George asked.

"So's I can see if I'm tellin' it right. I was once as blind as you are now, but I had to learn to see with my own eyes. I wondered about God's brand of justice, too. Some folks seem to have life pretty easy, but look down deep. You'll see God evens up the score more often than we 'spect. My boyhood wasn't unlike your own 'cept we didn't have schools like today . . .

The Fiddlin' Man's Story
of the Boy Who Lost God

I was aridin' home with Pa from church one Sunday. Right there in the spring seat in the wagon on a day that would make Indiana right proud to send up to heaven. And I was afidgetin' like all-get-out.

"What's got into you a sudden," Pa said as we stopped at the wooden crossbar gate that shut off the lane so the cows couldn't get out.

"I dunno," I answered as I hopped down to unbar the gate. The gate creaked open, its bottom cut a fan in the dust of the road. "I feel sorta dizzy in the head."

"Ailin'?" Ma leaned forward from her seat toward the back of the wagon. I pretended to dust off the crease of my Sunday pants when she caught me by the ear as I climbed back into the wagon. "You don't look so peaked. Sure you took that sulphur'n'lasses last spring?"

"Aw, Ma." I jerked away. "I'm not ailin'. It's just a feelin', a funny feelin' like I had a peculiar appetite fer somethin'."

"Well, Peter, long as you're just dizzy in the head is no cause to be fretted about. Jest natural." And Ma laughed like she always did when Pa made a joke.

As we stopped to let Ma out at the well gate, I hopped down, too, knowin' that if I didn't begin to look pert the castor oil bottle would be my reward.

When Pa unhitched the horses and came up toward the house he found me leanin' against the fence post by the orchard, twistin' the rusty points of the section of barbed wire. The sun was warm upon my scalp, and by shuttin' my eyes I could feel the warmth lull me to a sort of half-awake sleep. The wind was lazy with the scent of the pines, the firs, and with the blossoms of the new beans in the garden. There was a late call of a mournin' dove who just hadn't all his licks in for the day, and somewhere in the distance the bells of the cows pastured in the hollow sounded the knell of contentment. Below, in the creek hollow, a small animal was closin' in for a drink.

"Whatcha moonin' there fer?" Pa teased. "Six, or is it seven? Much too young to be love-sick." Pa went on up the path to the cabin. "Not long till eatin' time."

I waited a while afore tacklin' the path. My wool pants scratched my legs. My Sunday shirt and tie seemed to try a race to see which one could choke me first. Unused to low-cut shoes, I was bothered by the dirt that flushed in over the tops. I stopped to take my shoes off and shake them.

"Never knew you to be late fer a meal," Ma said as I stumbled in to the dark, sweet-smelling kitchen. "Hungry as a coon?"

"Not 'specially." I went to my room and closed the door behind me.

Wasn't long 'fore Pa came in and looked me over. "Don't bring that attitude to the table, Peter," he said. "Who'd want a sour face to spoil those chicken and dumplin's Ma's gonna serve up dreckly?"

"Me spoil 'em? I'm not tryin' to act up. Honest."

"Maybe you've no mind to, but when you get somethin' eatin' you, actin' up just comes natural."

"I don't mean to be contraryin', it's just that what's botherin' me I can't seem to talk about. Even to myself."

I stared down at my dusty shoes while hopin' all the while Pa would go away. He didn't. Instead he said, "Want to tell me about it?"

"Can't tell no one. It's just — just that I — well, I just don't believe in God." I blurted it out before I could grab my mouth.

The surprisin' thing was that Pa didn't act shocked. "Now that's what I call a hog-callin' fact. Since when has this been eatin' you? And how come?"

"Been botherin' me ever since I lost Him. Just can't seem to find Him. Been huntin' everywheres."

"'Pears to me a boy your age might be alookin' too hard." He sat down before the old wooden shelf where I kept my books and my oil lamp. "Tell me, where did you look? Jes' how did you hunt?"

"Well, at church, I guess. If He's anywhere, I guess He'd be there."

"And who was tellin' you that?"

"The preacher. Didn't you hear him say it was the Lord's house, and hear them sing about the Lord bein' in His holy temple?"

"That's true. Yet the Lord's got lots of houses 'side church."

"Wish He had a mind to stay home, then."

Ma summoned us all to dinner then, and Pa said, "Maybe you'd think better with some vittles in you. And you got a long road to travel. It all depends on you how long that road is."

When we sat up to the table Ma said, "Fixed this dinner special fer you, Peter, 'cause you been eatin' kinda puny of late. So eat every scrap."

"Sure smells good," I had to admit while tryin' to do justice to Ma's cookin'. Chicken just gold with dumplin's. Late lettuce in sweet vinegar. A mountain of new potatoes mashed with gobs of country butter makin' yellow streaks where it melted. Yeast rolls crusty to keep the warm steam inside until you opened one. The crystal jelly dish brim-full with the summer's first strawberry jam. What a long time Pa took sayin' grace!

"Think that lemon pie will be enough to jolt him out of his fast," Pa said to Ma with a wink.

"Don't see how all them people managed to fast in Bible times," I ventured. "How come they did it, Pa?"

"Fastin' was a kind of test. Sort of to test the spirit and flesh."

But after eatin', full as a colt in the soybean patch, I still didn't feel any closer to God fer havin' eaten. I went to my room and flopped on my straw-tick mattress. A long way to go, Pa said. Maybe it was like Pa said. Maybe I had been huntin' too hard. Maybe if I just waited God would get around to comin' to me. But that made me feel like a coward; for hadn't it been written: *Come unto me?* This left me more mixed up than ever. I remember that I doubled my knees up against my chest and prayed a frantic bit. "Lord, for my sake light someplace and stick around till I get there, won't you?"

I got tired of rollin' on the quilt after changin' my clothes, so I went outdoors. Surely that would be the place to look for God if I ever found Him. I listened to the rustlin' of the satin-green leaves of the oak tree by the garden fence. No God. I kicked a rock of the path and bent over to watch a grub worm wigglin' in the damp spot the rock left behind. No, God wouldn't be in a worm. God didn't hide under a rock. A chicken hawk buzzed against the sky over by the county road. No, God didn't fly around lookin' fer somethin' to pounce on. Guess I musta wasted several hours just huntin' God. 'Fore I knew it Ma was out in the chicken yard afixin' to feed table scraps to her chickens. I must have been a little tired when I started to walk over to the chicken pen, for I swayed into the fence. Ma turned, startled like, to say, "My, Peter, you do look a little sick. Better come on to the house."

"I'm not sick, Ma," I explained as the chickens flocked up,

peckin' at each other, to be fed. "I just wondered if you had time to talk a spell."

"A woman can take time to talk to her growin' son, I 'low." Ma paused while the chickens pecked the dish clean to look at me curiously.

I felt as awkward as a new calf. "Suppose you'd lost somethin', Ma. Where'd you go to hunt it?"

Ma looked bewildered. "That depends on what I'd lost. If it be a hen, why I'd look on the nest. What'd you lose, Peter?"

For the moment I'd wished to be turned into a hen just so I wouldn'ta had to answer. "Well, well, I — " I wavered while feelin' a sunburnin' blush creep up from my bare toes. "Well, some folks call what I'm lookin' fer — God."

"Oh, you mean our Lord?" she said just as if I'd been askin' 'bout our nearest neighbor over by Shakamak. "Why, He's all around!"

I stretched my skinny neck to look around me, clean out to the woodlot. "I sure would be pleasured to see!"

"You mean yer askin' fer proof? Be it so, I still say the hen's nest." She went on back to the house, leavin' me angry at myself fer bein' stupid enough to ask. Just plain angry.

I watched until she had disappeared into the house, and then I stole a quick look into the henhouse. Walkin' cautious-like, so's not to frighten a late-settin' hen, I reached my hand into the nest to feel the egg ol' Biddy had just laid. The egg was warm, so warm that I pulled my hand away like it had been burnt. And there was ol' Biddy out there eatin' again. Just like her life depended on it, so's she could get fat and lay more eggs for our table, and Ma could make more lemon pies for a boy to eat who had lost God and couldn't find Him . . .

God sure wasn't in the henhouse, I knew, so I walked on out to the barn lot where Pa was readyin' to do the evenin' milkin'. Pa had put the milkin' stool in place and was streamin' white cords of milk in a saw-saw rhythm into the shiny tin bucket. "Patty, you keep them legs still and that tail out of my face or you'll be the first bob-tailed Jersey in Genesis County, so help me!" Pa threatened.

"I'll milk for you, Pa," I offered. "Patty'll gentle fer me." The scent of the bran'n'shorts Patty chawed was as perfume in the barn with its clover bales overhead.

"Don't look as if you're pert enough to milk. Still can't find what you were lookin' fer?"

"No," I admitted hoping to gain sympathy there in the gathering dusk outside the barn door. "Farther away than ever."

"That's a good sign you're gettin' close."

Pa's words were tantalizin'. "If you know, I wish you'd tell me, Pa. If you *do* know . . ."

"I know all right, but every feller has to find the place by himself. Ain't no two people alike. Suppose you go back to that place where you first asked me this mornin' and take a good look around."

"You mean God's been there all this time at the gate. How'll I know He's there, ain't gone again?"

"How?" Pa asked in a voice verging on anger. "Likely He'll hit you in the face!"

"Face? Hittin' don't sound like God to me. And supposin' he don't?"

Pa waited a moment like he was gettin' ready to explode. "Then you stay right there until He does!"

I dared not disobey Pa, so I was off before he made up his mind to lay a hand on me. I slowed down afore I got to the gate, thinkin' it wouldn't be right to meet God all out of breath. I wondered what God would think of meetin' me with no shoes on, and looked over my shoulder a time or two just fer safety's sake. The burrs stuck to my pants but I stopped to pick them off. Still no God. The shadows of evenin' len'thened into ribbons of deep blue sky tyin' the earth into a neat package, a present to offer the moon. The way it looked I was gonna be there all night to listen to the frogs over on Shakamak. I tired of hangin' over the gate, and finally sat down on the rock that marks the fence boundary. The sky was beginnin' to wave colored handkerchiefs as a goodbye to the disappearin' sun; the crazy quilt of colors asked to tuck the earth in for the night. Then the moon, only as the fellow who wrote about the moonlight's fair tonight along the Wabash could describe it, hung out its sign that it was open for business. With the yellow paleness came the mist that hovers with the night in Indiana. The smell of the warm earth seekin' to cool itself under the shower of these mists was strong in my nostrils. A quail whistled someplace from a covey as a cricket began to tell how many stitches he'd made that day while tryin' to sew up the cracks in wood. The wind from the cabin brought the scent of honeysuckle; my heart beat with a strange sadness, a strange longin' to be back inside the cabin with my own kind, to be with those I belonged with. I shivered in spite of myself. A sharp wind blew up as I turned to look back toward the lamplighted cabin — hit me right in the face, it did. I tried to hold me breath to keep from knowing. For suddenly I knew. "Why this is it. This is Him," I said so sharply that I frightened a field mouse who didn't know I was near. "This is what Ma said about the nest, the warm egg. This is what Pa said about lookin' first in the place where I thought I lost Him; that He is everyplace; that it's somethin' a fellow has to know and to find out fer himself . . ."

I went back to the cabin with my head hangin' kinda low. I couldn't keep from grinnin' 'cause Ma and Pa looked at each other like they was mighty proud. Didn't have to explain nothin' to them — just like I'd been out doin' chores.

"Supper's in the warmin' oven," Ma said, lookin' up from the Bible she held on her lap. I peeked over her shoulder only long enough to see she was readin' 'bout the prodigal son; was mighty embarrassed that her eyes were wet.

Supper was still warm yeast rolls and chicken leavin's to gnaw on. Washed it all down with Saturday's churnin' of cool buttermilk. Not a feast, but to me it was pure manna. And I was Moses.

Uncle Pete finished his story in humility, the humility of a long-ago lesson recalled. He reached across to adjust the wick of the lamp and removed his glasses once more.

"It was right after that when Pa got the book of hymns and prayers that Johnny Appleseed carried when he was in Indiana.

In Pa's own hand he wrote on the flyleaf the riddle: What creature is it that in the morning of his life . . . ? Pa gave the book to me and told me to give it to my own kin I would someday leave behind me in Genesis County. It'll be yours, boy. Cherish it, for it is the missin' link of the sincere Eastern religion that made our country in the first place. It is of the Quakers and all the others who came to open up the West. Weren't much religion brought in 'cause men got too busy lookin' after their own interests. Johnny Appleseed, even though some people thought him a queer one, was a pioneer in his own way. Be proud of the book, George. Someday it will be valuable."

And there, in that room where all of Genesis County seemed hushed to listen to words of wisdom, George learned. In the sputtering lamp glow he asked, "And are the people coming Sunday to hear the myths retold? If they are I want to stick around and get all the facts straight."

"Facts?" The Fiddlin' Man smiled again to tease. "Why do you always want facts? Facts have been the undoin' of men many times over, George. I wouldn't say the Irish are a race of liars, mind you, but they have a little gift of adding fancy to the facts. And fancy never killed off near as many people as facts have. You'll find this out when you're older. Abe Lincoln didn't live far from here as a boy. There were a lot of *facts* in his life, but it'll be the *fancies* people will always talk about — this part of his life that made folks love him. Me, I remember the *fancies,* and other folks seem to, too, If this is wrong in the sight of man I kinda like to figure God kinda winks when our kind comes forward on Judgment Day."

The Fiddlin' Man didn't have to ask for an audience on Sunday afternoons. The people came in buggies, in wagons, on horseback, and the nearest neighbors on foot; a motley procession in clean denims and bonnetted calico gathered together to sit on the ground, under the shade of the giant oaks on the Homeplace, to listen to the stories about Indiana that he told. In a Godfearing community this form of recreation was tolerated and had become almost a tradition in Genesis County.

Sometimes the group was more than thirty. The narrator sat in an old chair with a broken arm, his back to the barrel-stave hammock. A hush fell over the crowd when he lighted his pipe to begin.

"Tell us about the Indian, Shakamak," one boy would beg.

Then, while George wrote furiously on a pad balanced on his crossed knees on the ground, the Fiddlin' Man began . . .

The Legend of Shakamak

There are many legends about our County. Some of them are based on facts. Some will swear they are the truth, just as some will swear that Owen County got its name from "Sweet Owen." It's true that Terre Haute once kept fort soldiers who gave it the name which means "high ground." But the legends differ about Genesis County which got its name from the Genesis Tree, called by some the Raintree. There's the story that a wealthy landowner imported the trees to plant beside his gates in an experimental project; for this reason people used to call them Gate Trees. Quakers and Miami warriors used to come from miles around just to stare at them, they say; for no one in Indiana ever had seen such splenderous buildin's about.

I guess it was only natural for someone to get the idea that the beautiful Gate Trees might be the same ones from the Garden of Eden, for they are mighty hard, nigh impossible, to start from seed.

Who brought the first Genesis Tree into our county? It's hard to prove, but my father, my own pappy who was the first preacher to come up here from the South in the early eighteen hundreds, claimed he brought it in. Claimed that the good Lord sent him a vision, told him to come into the Northwest Territory seeking a place where the Genesis Tree had originally come from, and that the tree would be the same one that came out of the Garden of Eden: the Tree of Life. He told him that wherever the tree took root that there man could make a paradise on earth if he wanted to make it one. My old pappy chose Genesis County, for here was Shakamak water with its beauty.

Once the Indians told their own story about Shakamak.

Shakamak, a handsome young Indian brave, whose Indian name meant "Long Eel," was as clever and as powerful as his name. His deeds of darin' had traveled throughout his territory so much that the young braves of other tribes and councils were jealous. The tribal lore brought young Shakamak stories of the beauty and cleverness of Princess Winona, the daughter of a chief of another tribe. And when Shakamak looked upon the face of Winona, he sighed and fell in love with her forever. All would have been well had not so many other young braves been in love with her too.

Winona's father wished to choose the best husband for his talented daughter. He decided on a test for Shakamak in order to win the Princess's hand, warnin' that if he failed in the task he would die. The chief ordered that Shakamak perform the task of bringing to the chief, as a gift, a treasure he had never seen before, and put a time limit on the days he was allowed to make his offering.

Winona wept because she was afraid that Shakamak's enemies, some in her very own tribe, would cause him to fail in the task. She knew that every move Shakamak made would be watched critically in order to do him harm, and she desperately wanted Shakamak to win her.

Realizin' that there was no time to be wasted, Shakamak dove into the water of a river which would take him to the shore where the Genesis Tree grew, for in his deeds of bravery he had heard about the tree. He swam the long distance which would have killed a lesser warrior, and sustained long punishment by spirits he met in the waters. The delays to overcome these evil spirits caused him to lose time. He arrived at that settlement during the night and could not raise anyone in order to ask for a branch of the golden tree. Without permission he broke a branch from the tree and began his long trip back home. Long before he reached home, Winona heard by the Indian drum messages what he had done.

Knowing full well that Shakamak's enemies would say he had defaulted by stealing the branch, Winona tried to seek another treasure that her father had never seen.

For many years the witch doctors had told about the "black diamonds" which would give much heat that were hidden below the earth's surface. Winona bravely entered an uncharted cave, which legend said descended into the heart of the earth, to search for this treasure her father had never seen.

When Shakamak returned, sure enough the Chief rebuked him for taking the branch without permission. Shakamak, once so proud of the beautiful branch of the tree he had sacrificed to bring as a present, and shocked with the news that Winona had probably sacrificed her life in order to help him, was broken-hearted. In his desperation and great grief, he flung the branch from him on the shore of the lake, and dove into the water to ask the spirits to help him to find Winona, his love.

But the evil spirits Shakamak had overcome in his fight in the river united to ruin him. While he was searching the water that flowed into the cave, the water rose up to flood the cave. But Shakamak was happy because inside the cave he was united with Winona, and they decided that it was best to desert their earthly form and be joined by the watery kingdom. They were both washed into the Lost River which flows underground in Orange County.

Legend says that one can often hear them laughing together at night, especially when other young human lovers sit beside the lakes and creeks in Indiana. And, if you listen close enough, you can hear their soft sigh of envy, wishing they were human once again. That's why Shakamak has such a legendary attraction for lovers.

❋

And long after the other listeners would depart on the Sunday afternoons, the boys who were friends of George would gather around him to reread the notes he had made in his notebook.

"Do you really think the legends happened just as Uncle Pete, the Fiddlin' Man, tells them?" Red Poe asked.

"Don't know why not," George replied after thinking a moment, his pencil between his teeth. "And I don't know but what Charlie, here, is right, too, when he says that the tales have just sort of wandered aimlessly from one generation in Indiana down to another. He's right. It's high time somebody kept a record for other people — so that they will know how things were in our times!"

"George, are you sure that's the same tree you found in the woods that day — the day we saw Cosey?"

"Sh-hh-h. That's not to be told about, understand," George warned the younger boy.

"I know." Red blushed as red as his hair.

"I hope to live to prove that the tree I found, there at the spot Shakamak was supposed to have thrown down his branch, is really the one spoken of in Genesis."

"How do you mean to prove it?" Charlie pushed back a forelock of hair so that he could see George's face in better light.

"Think I'll just start it and keep a record of everything I find out. Or maybe I'll work like one of those New York detectives. Could be I'll do like Columbus when he came over here to find America."

Red hugged his knees to his chest to rock over that statement. "You forget that Columbus wasn't looking for America, George. He was looking for China or India or something. He never was a success in that."

"That's right. It would have been worse yet if he had said, 'Look, Isabella, old girl, I'm afraid to go looking. You can keep your old leaky tubs. What do I care if God's word gets to anybody else or not? Do you think I want people laughing at me if I never prove the world is round?'" Charlie argued just to get a laugh.

"You got something there," Red answered as he chewed a weedstem. "I guess if Columbus hadn't discovered us, we'd all have slanting eyes and eat chop suey all day; but it's a fact that he didn't really find what he looked for so long."

George closed his notebook with a sigh. "No, Columbus quested in vain, and maybe I won't find positive proof — ever — that the Genesis Tree was the one in Eden. Maybe I can never be successful in getting a tree to sprout from one of those seeds — just as God gives life to us; but I aim to try. Hard."

"Hope you do, George," Red wished. "But ain't you a little bit afraid of running into that flaming sword it tells about in Genesis, the one God put up so no man could find Eden again?"

George pondered Red's question until the sound of quiet made itself noticed. "I guess there's a price we have to pay for everything. I reckon I'll have to be willing to pay the price, whatever it is . . ."

Genesis County is gashed with ravines, once washed by creeks of twisting, complaining water, cut between two hillsides which, opposite each other, send a code of echoes between them about the woods which crown their highest points skyward. Boyhood dreams of great adventure and daring are begun when a boy grasps the grapevine swing on one hill to swing out across the ravine to the other side. He never quite makes it, yet he is king while he is in the air; and what boy can really grow to manhood not knowing what it is like to be king, at least once?

Time swung away the hours of George's youth like the trip of the vine swing on the Homeplace, a trip out into breathless space. In his mind, as in the minds of all the other boys who tried it, was the premonition of sudden death. Always, though each of them would deny it to the others. Will this be the last time my feet leave the earth? Will this rush of wind, this fresh wind never felt by any other person before, as I swing out over the creek that divides this ravine, be the last feeling in this world? And why do I swing out at all — with only the rough, strong vine clasped between my hands and knees to save me from a downward plunge? Is this fear the price of the thrill of returning to earth which gave us life? Life is not unlike this. Each experience. Is it not the strayer, the darer to sin, who knows that he must eventually swing back to God, to the security of firm earth beneath his feet?

Like the hours on the swing, George's college days had gone as he poured hours into the study of the earth's secrets. Good, solid companies had offered him tremendous salaries if he would go to faraway places. Just as Thoreau was thought odd at Walden Lake, companies thought it odd that George would not forsake Genesis County to take jobs which would have meant much to his future.

"It's that I'm happier here," he would explain. "I have to search here for my kind of people."

The men in their neatly pressed suits, men representing oil and coal companies, would shake their heads in disbelief. "Among these people? Why, they're little better than hillbillies here. And wasting your time gathering up these myths? No one believes them! You, a grown-up, educated man, fooling around in woods taking state-offered jobs when you need money! What a waste." Then the men would go back to their shiny cars and slam the door. After consulting a road map to find their way to other possible employees from a list furnished by the university, they would leave Genesis County.

More and more of George's time was spent in the deep woods. During the summer, school-idled children followed him like the Pied Piper as he explained woods lore to them. (Most of the lore was based on the fact, but quite liberally tempered with fancy.)

In complete honesty sometimes, as they walked with him to take samples of rock from the creek beds, the children would speak on their favorite subject.

"How come you, past thirty now, never got married up with some nice gal and had kids of your own?" Tim took his turn. "Mommy says it's a mystery to her. Told Daddy those very words."

"Guess I'm not ready to settle down just yet," George laughed down at the tiny Tim whose hair was as yellow as sunlight and as rumpled as straw in a hen's nest. But it's nice to hear that your folks are concerned about me, Tim."

"My daddy say you would have if you didn't have a callin'.

And Mommy say 'A callin', you say? If you was to ask me it's an excuse to loaf and roam the woods all day instead of doin' his manly duties.' That you say you are trying to find out some secret about the Genesis Tree."

"And your mommy may be right," George laughed. "Seems I'm quite a topic for conversation, at least."

"I'll say you are, George." Sandy, the tomboy of the group, scratched the seat of her blue jeans as she admired the tall George. "But Dad holds up for you. Says that if you can really find out a secret about life from that ol' tree, you would give it away to everyone. Mom said — one day right when the preacher was callin' — that you loved God's earth here in Indiana almost as much as God did once when He — "

George interrupted as Sandy caught her breath. He lifted her from the ground and cradled all of her tender years against his chest, to search her honest eyes. "And what did the preacher say?" he begged, his voice drained white with all seriousness.

The swiftness of his action startled Sandy until she almost forgot. "The preacher? Oh, him. He said that God would punish you — hard; his eyes got all pushed together. He said you shouldn't try to find out God's secrets." Sandy kissed George's nose while laughing at the memory. "Then Daddy made a joke of it when the preacher left. Said 'Why George's got more religion in his little finger than that preacher's got under that shiny black vest.' That's just what Daddy said!"

George feathered the child to the ground as if she had been a cream pitcher, brim-filled, on a Sunday's table cloth.

Not to be unnoticed, Ellen Lot piped in her salty two-cent's worth. "My folks say it don't make any difference what you're lookin' for. They say they'd rather hear you tell your stories you write down in that notebook you carry than any radio program they ever heard. They love you, George! And Mom says that's what's important. She'd rather have you come visit us with your tales than Banker Bull with all his money. Says he ain't smiled for a week of Sundays, Bull ain't."

Then came the months that late winter that folks guessed

George was really on to something strange and mysterious. He went to the deep woods at dawn and stayed until dark, alone.

When his notebook was full he went to the drugstore for more fillers. The incident was discussed by the druggist at great length later on when he retold it.

"Not got the kind you usually buy, George," the portly druggist, a Methodist deacon, explained. "But let me sell you some of this fancy kind, rainbow paper we got special for the Easter season. See, it's got each page marked with a cross and an Easter lily, that's for the beginnin' and the end, see? That's 'cause they rolled the stone away when Jesus was supposed to be buried, killed on the cross like on the paper. But take the lily, now. That's pure new life comin' on after death. If anyone was to ask where you got that filler, you might mention my drugstore, you know. It's a new item. A forty-cent value for a quarter. Mighty pretty colors — pink, yellow, blue, and green like a rainbow of promise. And seein' that cross and lily, the symbols of life and death, ought to help evangelize people. Make 'em stop and think at the same time . . ."

No one ever learned just exactly what George was doing in the woods that day. Maybe he had at last learned the secret of starting a Genesis Tree from seed, but the Bible had said it *couldn't* reseed itself. There was never any proof, but some thought that he had seen a tiny sprout when he lifted that tin can from the ground, for he still had the can in his hand when they found him that morning there at the root of the Genesis Tree.

. . . The stillness around him there in the spring dusk of evening was as primitive as it had been that day so long ago before time began in that other woods around Eden. Why is it so still? his heart asked his body, paralyzed by the discovery. There is no wind, no twittering of birds scolding their young at nightfall. The lake below is rippleless; no stir of feet walking upon the waters. Is devotion to purpose, devotion to searching for God, the anwser? Is that the secret of Life or of re-creating it from seed? Is it really life I see beneath this can? Or do my eyes, blind with my desire to know, deceive me? Have I learned to be tolerant of man — have dared to search for Truth — so that God has shown he one of His secrets? . . .

And there on his knees he learned, perhaps, what Moses learned so long ago from a burning bush. "Oh, God . . . Oh, my God . . ." he whispered in his ecstasy of knowledge.

It wasn't until the next day that Jacob Saul, searching for a lamb lost from his flock, found George's body.

"In all my seventy-three years, I've never seen lightnin' come up in the woods like that without a sign of storm until that huge crack of it come. I remember remarkin' to my wife Sarah last evenin' when the lightnin' cut across the sky, 'Biggest flash I ever seen!' Must have been that one that hit him. Split that Genesis Tree — and I never knowed one was alive in this county — down the center. Burned it and the ground around it to a crisp. The roots, topsided to the ground, just powdered in my hand. What made it most peculiar was that down in the hole the roots had left, I found the lamb, not even black, safe as anything! Jest like it was left in all its innocence to mark the place!

"I went straight to the lake road to get help from the sheriff and to call George's folks. While I was awaitin' I went back and found that notebook George always carried. The myths he wrote on the white paper were still there, but the part where he had added the fancy, colored paper was all burned away. S' funny thing how the lightnin' jest burned away the words he was writin' then and left the rest. A funny thing. Jest like it was all planned away ahead of time. Gives a man a scary feelin', don't it?"

Then, in a tone meant by neighborly love to be kind, he added to Bonnie and Jay Miller, the distant cousins of George, "Folks is mighty curious about the queer way George was called home. But everyone loved him. Grownups and kids. It was like he was kin to all of us, somehow. God couldn't of called a better man, now could He?"

The curiosity of the people was but normal under the circumstances, and George left his books of tales and his book that Johnny Appleseed carried as his estate. One of the first to confirm that George was a good man, and also the first to introduce the mystery about how he died into every conversation, was

PART THREE

Miss Cosey Walters

Every small town has its busybody. All searchers hunt for reasons why people find pleasure in gossiping. Some find great humor; some find pathos; some find need. Often that rare combination is embodied in one person. Through it all shines the need for existence, the need to feel wanted, and the need of substituting it for the one purpose of having lived. Writers and artists attempt to bring this mystery of human behavior into the light so that everyone can see and understand, but often no one cares enough. And when no one cares enough, we will find a bit of ourselves, and a bit of everyone we have known, in Genesis County. Here we will find . . .

MISS COSEY WALTERS

IT ALL BEGAN that October evening in 1917 when Coseth Eve Walters visited her mother's grave to plant a Rose of Sharon bush. Cosey, as she was called in Jakeyville, Indiana, had fancied herself, at seventeen, in love with the elderly late Dr. Starbuck, and had helped herself to the bush from his estate. Cosey felt justified. "Hadn't Doc left his old house and grounds to be sold for a hospital's benefit?" she argued as she slipped into the grounds that night to dig up the bush.

But it wasn't a theft-sense of guilt that stamped this night as indelible on her memory. It was what she saw, heard, and felt in that Green Valley graveyard which changed her life. "It was," as Cosey described it later, "enough to make the hands of the clock in the Genesis County Courthouse hide its face in shame!"

Cosey had come carrying her booty, the bush, into her front yard that night before it all happened.

"That's stealin' fer sure!" Cosey's father, Buck Walters, warned in greeting. The porch swing creaked with the weight of the scolding, middle-aged miner. Cosey ignored him and placed the bushes on the dusty ground beside the sagging porch. The house listened in gray silence to the never-ending argument.

"What you want with them old clutter-uppers, anyhow? Beats me all holler. Them bushes don't belong to you nohow." He shifted his corncob pipe, held between the rows of yellow, worn teeth, and spat out over the banister. A cricket, disturbed by the *plop* sound, chirped in protest.

"Why ain't the bushes same as mine?" Cosey asked while she tucked her pink-striped shirtwaist into her navy blue hobble skirt. "Doc would have gave them to me while he was alive if I had asked."

"But you didn't ask. Now Doc's deader'n a door nail, and his propitty's gone up fer sale."

"Not to me Doc ain't dead. So takin' the flowers ain't a sin long as I'm plantin' some on Ma's grave. They wouldn't bring enough to buy a slop jar fer that there hospital as gets his leavin's."

Cosey was slender and well formed for her seventeenth year. Her skin was freckled; acne had left a few faint scars on her forehead and chin. Her nose, large with narrow nostrils, did not improve her face. Her full lips were her pride; she used them often, while quite young, to exaggerate pronunciations, and for their effect on the ever elusive male when she was fourteen — an age when most of Jakeyville's girls were old enough to know what lips were for. When Cosey was nervous, she crooked a forefinger to hold it against her upper lip, where faint hair grew, to feel pleasure and assurance from the pressure. Now this accusation by her father made her nervous. She sought escape, her finger at her mouth.

"I'm goin' out to plant the Rose of Sharon direc'ly," she said, hoping he would object and save her the trip up the Green Valley Road to the graveyard. Maybe Trixie Myers will come along with me."

"Trixie mighten," he encouraged, although he was not afraid for Cosey to make a trip like this alone. " 'Ceptin' I wouldn't want your best friend Trixie to know you stole them bushes from ol' Doc's."

"Oh, Trixie wouldn't care." Cosey's tone was much wiser than her years. "We understand each other. About Doc, I mean."

"The way you talk!" he growled. "People'll think things about you 'at ain't nice. After you moonin' around after Doc like you did. They'll think I neglected my duty, since your ma's gone on, asettin' you straight."

Cosey let the matter drop as she selected a bush with one hand and grasped the light spade with the other. Cutting triangularly across their back yard, past the coal shed and the outhouse, to the Myers' house across the alley, she mumbled to herself. "A lot he knows about me and Doc!" The moon seemed to mock with a laugh the lie she was imagining for the moment. "Trixie knows all about the affair between me and Doc down by the boathouse. He didn't have a woman to look after him in all those twelve years, did he? And didn't he need me? I'll say. Someday when Trixie's no longer my best friend, I'll make her eat her words for laughin' at me when I made up that story about me and Doc down by his boathouse!"

She entered the walk which bisected the Myers' back yard. Next door Maggie Bickle was busy, clothespins in her mouth, taking her day's washing from the line in the dark. Six Bickles, and one more on the way, kept Maggie over a washboard for hours, many of them after sundown.

"Callin' after Trixie?" Maggie volunteered. "She left afore dark with one of them Wilson boys."

This news left Cosey with two choices. Either to go alone to the graveyard, or to return home to face her father's accusations of stealing the shrubs, was little choice. But since her father would tease her, saying that Trixie always seemed to find pleasant company with boys when Cosey couldn't, she chose the trip to her mother's grave, a trip of slightly less than two miles.

Main Street ended at Enoch's Corner Hardware Store. Cosey turned left at Shem Street, walked the nine blocks to where the shale road began, then left the path to battle the ruts. In the yards of the houses, small, so-alike shacks built by the coal company to house its miners' families, broken chairs and porch swings were strewn. The nip of the early Indiana fall had driven people inside the shacks and early to bed; the early shift called for four-o'clock risers.

Cosey was glad that these prying eyes did not disturb her trip. Otherwise she would have had to answer those who asked, from their dark porch swings, "Why, where you goin' this time o' night?" There were *those* kind of people in Jakeyville who didn't think her simple explanation would be proper. Nice girls just didn't go out alone at night.

When Cosey reached the cut-off where the wheels of buggies and the hearse belonging to Boadie Boniran, the undertaker, had cut a road leading up the hill, she rested the spade on the ground before undertaking the climb.

That Boniran! Cosey remembered as the path grew steeper. Wasn't it common talk about the women Boniran had chased all over the county? Hadn't her own father joked with other miners, on payday nights down at the Last Chance Saloon, about Boniran burying all the men, and with each shovelful of dirt thrown back into the grave promising to take care of the widow left behind? "The Chinless Wonder," they had called him because Boniran's lower jaw receded almost into his Adam's apple. "Maybe they like Boadie's mustache," they kidded while winking knowingly at each other. Before the next round of beer was pushed, in sticky, wet mugs across the tables past the bowl of pretzels, one miner would be sure to crack: "Ol' Boadie keeps 'em all happy 'ceptin Miss Lucy, I'd reckon. Miss Lucy's never made a hat in her shop to fit him yet, but Boadie keeps hopin', that's for sure!"

Cosey could feel warmth spread to her throat whenever she heard a disparaging remark about Miss Lucy Shepheard who owned the town's best millinery shop. Lucy was a green-eyed, dark-haired beauty who had built a good business because she kept abreast of fashions — almost as late as those in the Sears Roebuck catalogue, her toughest competition in Jakeyville. Cosey, since her own mother had passed away, could easily pretend that her mother would have looked, if she had lived, a good bit like Lucy; that was why Cosey always made it her business to pass Miss Lucy's shop on the way home from school.

Often, as she paused to admire the hats mounted on inverted glass vases in the window, she could see Boadie Boniran loafing inside. He *must* have a good reason, Cosey told herself, for anyone who knew Miss Lucy knew that she was definitely not *that* kind to be — well, *fast,* if you had a mind to come right out and say it — or to have anything to do with the dapper undertaker!

Miss Lucy's interest in the undertaker was only harmlessly normal. Jakeyville's women got tired of looking at men with beards and dirty, broken fingernails, those who smelled of the carbide lamps which, fastened to their caps to light their way when working deep down in the damp, dark coal pits, reeked with unescapable fumes; and of the black-creased wrinkles in their faces and necks which no amount of strong yellow soap seemed able to remove entirely. That's why women made such a fuss over the physicians, the druggists, the teachers, the preachers, and yes — the undertaker, because they had clean hands and wore celluloid collars; that and no other.

As Cosey silently entered the open gate of the iron fence which surrounded the graveyard that night, the unexpected murmur of subdued voices frightened her. In the spasmodic periods of moonlight, she sought and located the black Boniran buggy outlined against a clump of vines which grew, covering the fence. Boniran's bay mare pawed the ground to let the buggy's occupants know that she waited impatiently.

Without knowing why she did it, Cosey looked around for concealment possibilities. In five more steps toward a sheltering bush, she dropped to her knees on the damp earth to eavesdrop and observe unseen the couple who cuddled in secret in the buggy.

The everchanging wind caused the leaves to rustle often, but when it sent its small gust her way, the voices carried. She recognized Boadie Boniran's familiar high-pitched, chinless-wonder voice.

"Now Lucy girl, you know I still care for you. No argument about that again, please. But I'm a respected man hereabouts, got a respectable family and my business. Getting a divorce would ruin me forever. You're crowdin' thirty, old enough to know that."

"Yes. I know ah-all th-that," Miss Lucy sobbed before the wind changed.

For almost three agonizing minutes Cosey waited for the wind to blow additional bits of conversation into her recording ears. A field mouse scuttled from his hiding place to the safety of a hole in the ground, yet Cosey refused fright and remained motionless.

"I'm known as a generous man, Lucy." The wind blew the impatient whine of Boniran's voice across the graveyard. "And I'm willin' to provide for your baby. But a name's out of the question, unless —"

"No. I don't want to marry that horrid Andy Johnston! He's simple, Boadie, you know that. Even if you could buy him into marryin' me."

"It's the only way for the baby to have a name!" he reminded in a voice with the serpent's sting in it. "An' since you insist on stayin' right here in Genesis County, it's the decent thing —"

"Dece — decent thing? Why you wouldn't know a decent th-thing . . ." Miss Lucy's pride, her disappointment, and her shame faded into the gust of wind which came from nowhere and went back again.

> *And the serpent said unto the woman, Ye shall not surely die: For God doth know that in the day ye eat thereof, then your eyes shall be opened, and ye shall be as gods, knowing good and evil . . .*

Cosey remained kneeling, in shocked stupor, as Boniran's buggy wheeled past her on its secret way back to town. Her back was arched into a cramp. She held her breath until her lungs ached in fear that the buggy's occupants would discover her hiding place and guess that she had overheard their conversation.

Then, with the buggy and its creaking wheels safely out of sight, she arose to plant, with numb fingers, the Rose of Sharon bush on her mother's grave. Her hands were cold but she didn't notice, at least not until one warm tear fell upon her right hand and another rolled down the spade handle to disappear on the damp earth.

"Why am I crying?" she asked herself. "About Miss Lucy? Why, what's happened to her has happened hundreds of times before around here. Katie Anderson's had four brats; two of them by the same railroad man, and nobody died over it . . ."

Cosey leaned forward on the spade to rest. Just as she tucked her blouse inside her skirt once more, a hoot owl challenged her reasonings with "Who-o-o-o?"

And Cosey paused to reconsider. No, Miss Lucy wasn't Katie Anderson who came from the long line of Andersons of Jakeyville — all alike. She was not like Katie. She was *Miss Lucy,* not like Katie at all! "You want to know 'who,' you ornery thing?" she flung at the unsuspecting owl who had asked in innocence. "Miss

Lucy's who, that's who! And I hate that God-forsaken chinless wonder who'd do a thing like that to her, that's why. And I wish I had him, had him right here in this place, right now. I'd show him what he is with this here spade. I'd . . . I'd . . ." Her anger gave way to tears; she sat down on her mother's gravestone. The stone held two clasped hands. The epitaph read: REST IN PEACE.

And God made . . . the lesser light to rule at night . . .

"Oh Ma, oh, Ma," she cried. "Why does life have to be this way? Why did it have to be her, and her so good, so pretty . . ."

The echo came back, just as it comes back from all of the years gone by, "Oh Ma, oh, Ma . . ."

"Lucy must have loved him," Cosey argued as she wiped her eyes on her petticoats made from feedsacks. "How could she be so simple, though? Just how?"

The owl, after a pause, asked his unanswered question again. "Who-o-o-o?"

"Stop it, dern you!" Cosey threw a clod of shale from the road at her unseen enemy. "If you're so daggone wise, why don't you do somethin' 'side askin'? I don't know either."

And Cosey didn't know after that. She didn't know why the spade was heavier as she walked down the hill on her way home. She didn't know why the wind seemed to moan instead of sing in the fir trees as she passed. She didn't know why the moonlight lost whiteness, nor why her button-shoes felt weighted. Was it because faith and hope, the brick and mortar to build the ivory tower, had not withstood the weathering of human fraility? Was this why each load would seem heavier now? Truth had yielded to the shifting winds. Good people were not good; things were not as they appeared on the surface. Everyone was bad. No, that wasn't true. Miss Lucy wasn't bad; it was that Boniran . . . just like a man . . .

In sorrow shalt thou eat of it all the days of thy life . . .

But if that were true, that a man is to blame, why did girls like Trixie desert her to go out in the company of a boy like that Danny Wilson? Why did girls giggle and preen before a mirror? Was there some strange secret to it all? There must be something nasty, she was certain. But yet Miss Lucy had loved . . . yes, she must have loved . . . well, no boy would ever make *her* meet him in any old graveyard. Ending up with a coal-miner husband and a house full of young ones wasn't for *her,* she decided.

As for Miss Lucy's secret, wild horses would never drag the story from Cosey's sealed lips. Not even if Miss Lucy had ten babies, none of them with chins, would she tell about the scene in the graveyard. She owed Miss Lucy that much, didn't she. All of the miners and their wives in Jakeyville were good people, but the town would talk as it had always talked. This time the talk would be worse, not like those Katie Anderson times. Maybe Miss Lucy would leave town. Maybe no one would ever know it if she married Andy Johnston. Maybe. But the crowd at the First Baptist Church would pry and ask her about it; so would those from the First Methodist. But Miss Lucy's secret was locked forever in silence.

Miss Lucy's secret would become a riddle to join the other riddles of the county. Cosey's promise, made to the heavens and pinned there on God's Bulletin Board by a star, would be a reminder of faith kept with Miss Lucy. The rainbow had been set in the cloud; the covenant would not be broken, at least until that time in Cosey's frustrated life when . . .

Now . . .

THE SERPENT WAS MORE SUBTIL . . .

The four girls, in locked-arm couples, were walking home from school that late November day. Jennie Hawroth and Mary Goss walked in front of Cosey and Trixie. The flurry caused by the arrival of the mailman's buggy coming in from the rural route was hushed in comparison to the state of excitement shared by the girls.

"And was I surprised when Danny up and offers me the ring," Trixie repeated for the umptieth time while holding her left hand out in front of her. " 'It's my mother's,' he said so sweet while my head spun around like waltzin' down at the Miners' Picnic last summer."

Pure envy, green as the pasture land in Genesis County in April, struck lightning in Cosey's narrowing eyes.

Trixie sensed the announced thunder with satisfaction. "I'll not be the first one married out of our class, but I'm the first one engaged." Honey of triumph seemed to drip from her serpent-wised lips. "Just think. No more carryin' school-lunch pails for me, soon."

"That's right," Cosey agreed. "Soon you'll be afixin' pails for your coal-mining man. The Wilsons are all pit men, you know." Her words were as disguised as poison ivy, glorified by red-green foliage and nourished by the earth's sweetest soil; yet when one brushed against the evil leaves, he had only to wait awhile to reap the sting and pain, the result of brief contact.

"Well!" Trixie stopped walking so that all could hear; the itch was already eating at her flesh. "You're just talkin' sour grapes, Cosey Walters! There's nothin' wrong with bein' a coal miner like each of our fathers were. Are you Rachel waitin' for a seven-year-Jacob? You just think you're somethin', that's all. Or are you still waitin' around for a professional man? Someone like ol' Doc Starbuck, maybe?"

Trixie's words reaped mocking giggles from the other girls.

Encouraged, Trixie sank her fangs yet deeper. "You just wait, Cosey. With that skinny, big nose, and your ways, you'll never get a man, let alone a miner. There's never a cowardly miner left alive in Genesis County, so there! You're just jealous 'cause I'm gettin' all the attention, the presents, and the church women's makin' me a quilt. Wouldn't you like to be me? Or do you think you can do better? Why don't you try?"

What is in words that churn, burn, spurn, learn, and turn? They are cruel in intent and more cruel by implication, yet no word is as painfully cruel to the hearer as the plain-truth-word uttered by a friend. Trixie's words scratched into Cosey to fester, boil up, and to overflow until Cosey felt she would drown in the flood of them. How could she redeem herself in front of her friends? Imagine how this incident would be magnified and reported to others inside the various homes in Jakeyville tonight! What would the boys at school say? Would they stand in front of Japeth's Pool Room and taunt her as she walked by? Would she be made a laughingstock? . . .

Cosey swallowed her bite of Pride's-apple; the taste was as bitter as tansy in a mess of spring greens. Somehow, some way, she must word her defense to regain Trixie's friendship, yet not appear to humble herself.

"I didn't mean for you to get so touchy," Cosey half apologized. "Between me and the gatepost, guess I could get me a boy as good as Dan Wilson after me if I had a mind to," she bragged a healing balm.

The expressions on the faces of the girls told her that her attempt at bravery had been as worthless as a mess of pottage. How could she redeem herself? What could she invent, say, or tell to direct interest away from her predicament?

Cosey tried again. "I . . . I mean . . . I guess I *know* a thing or two."

"Like that big fat hog lie about you and ol' Doc down at his boathouse, Cosey?" Mary Goss teased on, delighted with her success in making Cosey squirm. "You're always makin' up some tale like that. You'd run like Fry's red bull was after you if you ever came near to such goin's on!"

Cosey was pinned to a wall by their taunts. Anger as a viper spreading within her made the waistband of her skirt become, suddenly, too tight. She hadn't minded them calling her "Big Nose" before. Why, no one is perfect. But now the combination, that she was physically, sexually wanting, crowded caution beyond the line of danger. Hadn't she promised herself to keep a lifetime of silence about Miss Lucy's misfortune? Could she pay the price of her silence now that her friends salted her wounded pride?

Cosey closed her eyes to provide a second of escape. Had all of this happened before in other times? Had Jupiter driven Pandora to open *that* box to release evil into the world? Had Atalanta been tempted to pause in her race against her lover to pick up the golden apples given by Venus? And hadn't God asked, in an earlier Genesis County, only to be answered: "Am I my brother's keeper?"

The great need of the present — to redeem herself in the eyes of her friends — was too much. "I'm not makin' up tales," Cosey defended. "At least not in everyone's opinion."

Hating herself for her weakness, Cosey carefully weighed her words to make the awed attention, gifted to her by the girls, last longer. Juliet was in her balcony scene; Orpheus could not resist a backward glance and lost Eurydice; the serpent became beautiful in Eve's sight. Cosey took a deep breath and plunged. "I know who's going to have a baby, soon." She paused to give the girls time to check their mental-filed gossip lists.

"Who, Cosey?" Trixie begged, wanting to be friends again. "And is the girl married?" No beagle dog ever nosed closer to a warm trail.

"Not yet." Cosey glowed as she dangled clues to enhance the spice of her secret. "But I think she's goin' to be." Her lips parted at the anticipation of the pleasure and attention she was rating from them.

"Tell who, please!" Jennie implored as she shifted her stack of leather-strap-bound books so that she could stand nearer to Cosey.

"Someone we all know. I really shouldn't tell . . ."

Atalanta was tempted to continue the race, but the golden apple was too enticing. The apple on the Tree of Life glistened like a cluster of grapes after a shower in Genesis County.

"But tell us who she's goin' to marry. That much," Mary begged.

"Well," Cosey deliberated for a delicious moment, tasting the precious drop of popularity which sweetened her tongue, "It's Andy Johnston."

"Andy Johnston!" Mary challenged. "Who beside a baboon would marry that half-idiot with not enough sense to come in out of the rain? You're lying again, Cosey Eve Walters!"

"No, I'm not!" Cosey had placed her head into the noose so that thereby hangs the tale. The once-tempting coil of rope was swinging her so high that her feet dangled beneath her. She struggled in a sacrificial effort to get her feet back to the firm earth. "It's Miss Lucy Shepheard, that's who."

The web was spun from the frayed edges of the noose-rope. The web descended, confining at first; yet Vulcan, who designed Apollo's chariot, could not have done a better job in converting the ugly web-threads into strands of silver and gold. The web became a net of beauty. And Cosey lacked strength to escape while the serpent urged her to rest awhile.

World War I and the Kaiser's goat were discussed with less interest in Jakeyville homes that night.

As a result Cosey found herself a much honored guest at dinners and suppers; each hostess begged for firsthand *repeats* of the graveyard scene. Again and again Cosey enjoyed her new prestige like a hungry hound pup at butchering time; it didn't matter if the choice loin meat was sacrificed and taken away to be saved for times of more appetite, the bloody intestines were filling for the time being.

The hills and valleys of Genesis County magnified the echo until Cosey was immune to the arrows of Conscience when she invented particulars which did not exist except in her increased ability as a storyteller. She became willing to let her ear for news supplant her lack of sex appeal. (Boniran called her a snooping busybody.)

But to her secret, bitter sorrow, she learned the price for such a dubious talent: boys managed to keep a safe distance between themselves and this kiss-and-tell pigeon. Even in Genesis County there is a holy ground which no one invades; each man's body, his dreams, and his loves are his own secret treasure. The Lord is in His holy temple; Apollo still drives the chariot between the earth and sky.

Loneliness was a leech draining away her blood as Cosey ate of her own vanity. Ain't a one of Genesis County's boys good enough for me, anyway, she told herself as, one by one, the girls in her class were married "off" to miners. Manna was her substitute for flesh.

During that summer and the next she visited each girl in her newly established home to envy the swelling which announced a new life was being God-sent to Genesis County, or to cuddle the small bundle of joy which chose to suck his or her thumb as the baby was held close to Cosey's emptiness. Sitting on a friend's front porch, holding a blanket around a pale, wrinkled head to protect it from the late summer gusts, she would build enthusiasm into her envy-hiding words.

"I got a great callin' ahead of me instead of this. I'm goin' to Terre Haute Normal comes the fall. Goin' to teach . . ." And maybe, she secretly promised herself, I'll come across a man teacher up there. One who would appreciate me . . .

That was why Buck Walters, Cosey's father, went down to the red brick, narrow-celled Jakeyville Bank, on the corner of Main and Hulman Streets, to inquire about getting a loan from Mr. Andrew Lincoln Lamprey, the president. "Need the money to educate that gal of mine," Buck explained in the loan-asking room which was fenced off by wooden railings from the main room of the bank. His statement was unnecessary; Lamprey had heard the news earlier that day in the post office.

Andrew Lincoln Lamprey leaned back in his wooden swivel chair, which squeaked when he turned his profile to Buck, while he considered the loan. With his thumbs tugging as his vest pockets, Lamprey closed his beady but alert eyes which glowed beneath his heavy steel-gray eyebrows. Buck's assets stacked, one upon the other like a pile of silver dollars, in the coffer of Lamprey's mind. The mortgage on the house; its furnishings — the heating stove would bring a good twenty dollars any day; the fifteen acres of pasture land with the spotted heifers, some to freshen soon, grazing upon them; the sow with a butchering litter grunting over the yellow nubbins on the scattered ears in the barnyard; all these added up to enough to make a risk worth while. Andrew Lincoln Lamprey drummed pink fingertips, which looked odd in contrast with the blue-veined wrinkles of his brown hand, on the edge of his roll-top desk. When he cautiously peeled a drawer open to search for, with his fingertips, a loan form, he unfolded it to point out the lines where signatures were required — to "guarantee payment, of course," before turning to face the anxious Buck.

Room and board were Cosey's greatest expense at Terre Haute Normal; to solve this problem she found a job as a maid with the Markle family during her after-school and weekend hours.

Cosey's first year was barely completed when her father fell down the cellar steps of Widow Badder's house, the same widow who was known to keep an ample supply of home brew in that cellar. Buck broke his left leg. Cosey left school for the summer.

In October of that year Harriet Letzinger gave up her job at Redroof School to marry a tombstone salesman who stopped regularly in Jakeyville to spend the night at Bella Tennis's Boarding House. The vacancy created a problem for Trustee Andrew Lincoln Lamprey; in weighing his problem he considered the amount of the loan Buck Walters still owed the bank. Diplomatically, Cosey was hired even though her degree was still to be earned. Lamprey would see, of course, that the balance of the loan was taken from her salary, and that she would continue her education by taking summer courses at Normal.

Her permit to teach was extended again and again for many concocted reasons. But, after ten faithful years, the Board gave Cosey her reward, a permanent position as a full-fledged teacher in Genesis County, Indiana. Her days were as full as her nights were empty, but Cosey did her best to fill her empty arms by adopting to her heart the children of her former schoolmates from Jakeyville High, miners' children and all.

> . . . Urns are made empty only to be filled. The time of filling, the anticipation of being of service, is one of great effort. When, after struggle, the urn is filled to overflowing, reflection reigns. What of life is spilled over to stain the white cloth of purity beneath it? What is this joy when "my cup runneth over"? Does it serve to moisten Genesis County's . . .

GREENER PASTURES?

MR. POE, the civics teacher, was the first to hear early in 1927 that the Board had hired Mr. Adam Sappington, from Kokomo High School, up north, as the new superintendent. Cosey pumped from Mr. Poe all available information. In repeating the story she added a few details such as personal appearance and "what teachers who worked for him said." The news spread like chaff in threshing time.

Curiosity overwhelmed Cosey. When an advertisement for *World Books* came in the mail, she took the envelope to Mr. Andrew Lincoln Lamprey. Filled with Didn't-our-bank-make-her-education-possible pride, Mr. Lamprey gave Cosey additional information on Adam Sappington. Fired like a shot in a deep drilling, Cosey's interest set up a chain reaction. She packed her bags for a visit to Cousin Leah who, by strange coincidence, lived in Kokomo. No one in Jakeyville was surprised at Cosey's suddenly planned visit; Cousin Leah, who had not heard from her for seven years, however, was.

After a week had passed, Cosey returned to Jakeyville with information filed on little cards which she kept in her And-did-you-know category. She spread the details in teasing-sized morsels upon listening bread and served it to the many hearers of the Ladies' Aid Society, the Wives of Local Number Forty-seven, the Eastern Star, the Pocahontas Lodge, and just anyone who was willing to swallow, crust and all.

Did her interest in news carry her away? People thought so when she told that she forgot, in her great haste, to water her African violets, a duty she considered no less than a mother feeding her children. Was there some interests in this man besides news, apple-polishing, or job-promotion? More than one member of many families whispered, after Cosey's broad back had disappeared down a front walk, "It's too bad this Sappington has a wife and four children. He'd have been a natural man for Cosey to hitch to, wouldn't he now?"

Sappington's arrival was the subject of conversation all the way up from Shem's Barber Shop, where the son of Lucy and Andy Johnston was employed as a shineboy, to the Thursday night choir rehearsal at the newly built Lutheran Church.

Cosey managed to wangle an invitation to the Methodist Missionary Society's Luncheon. The potato salad, better than usual this time, was neglected by the fork she daintily paused above her plate.

"And Mr. Sappington, such an influential man upstate in teachers' organizations and P.T.A., will bring some changes to our school system. I'm to have the sixth, seventh, and eighth youngsters over at Redroof all by myself. The buses will pick up the younger ones to take to Miss Sarah Wusnidge's keeping over at Tater Hill. That way we'll have more time for each class. With our children multiplying so fast in number, we're going to have to build more schools to accommodate them all." She paused to nibble a bite from her ham-salad sandwich.

Bella Tennis grabbed her opportunity to get the attention of the group seated at the long luncheon table. "Redroof's scarcer than a mile from your house, Cosey, and less than a mile from the high school by way of Miller's Woods and the Eden Swamp land. You won't have to drive now, so that Ford coupé of yours will spend more time in your garage than it did last winter."

"I don't know about that," Cosey answered. "I hope so, 'cause it took lots of trouble and money to keep that Ford running when I went to Tater Hill last year. And a girl my age — with no man to fall back on — has to watch her nickles and dimes."

Bella let Cosey's reference to "girl" slip by. "Don't know what you'd want with a man, anyway," she said. "As much running around as you get done, a husband would be a hindrance."

"That's right," Cosey agreed as she took a fork to cut into the gingerbread desert on the extra plate in front of her. "I just never found time to get married." She laughed to prove to the others that she wasn't jealous. "If I did, it would have to be to another teacher like myself, one who was interested in culture and the better things of life."

"Someone like Mr. Abel Shultz who substituted for Mr. Wolfe that winter, maybe?" asked Opha Boston, the newest wife to join the group. (Opha, until her recent move to Jakeyville, had lived in Terre Haute and couldn't understand why Bella kicked her under the table to warn her to stop questioning Cosey.)

"Mr. Schultz? Oh, him?" Cosey made every effort to shade her face with mock disconcern. "Wouldn't have had him on a stack of Bibles. He was nice and all that, but those kind of men need a lot of mothering and straightening out. He never once darkened a church door in both of those months he was here, you remember?"

"Why, I heard you liked to run him — "

Bella awarded the honest Opha another kick, in the opposite shin this time, to shut her up; then Bella drowned out Opha's remark with: "A man who won't go to church is no man at all — at least one to look out for if you can, I always say."

The women, wise that Bella was craftily leading Cosey on, nodded to each other with amusement.

"Exactly my feelings, Bella." Cosey warmed to her opportunity. "But I sighed in relief when Mr. Schultz went back to his own school. He was pleasant company those few times he took me to the teachers' meetings, but mark my word, Mr. Schultz couldn't hold a candle to this Adam Sappington who's coming here. He's got polish, a program, and acts as a man with an education should. I know you good Christian mothers of our children are going to make him welcome. We teachers plan to do just that."

The women cleared the table after Cosey left. "Why did you kick me under the table, Bella?" asked the newcomer Opha as she gathered crumbs.

"You weren't here when Mr. Schultz substituted for one of our teachers, but the way Cosey chased him made us feel sorry for the poor guy. He was a little on the scared, mousy type anyhow. When Cosey started to sharpen her talons in his directions, he made tracks."

"That's just how I heard it, too," Opha giggled. "I was dumb there at first. How was I to know you where just egging Cosey on to see how far she would go? It's too bad she can't find a man as eager to marry as she is, I do declare."

"The pitiful thing is that she acts so desperate," Bella confided as she unloaded glasses into the kitchen's sink. "She ran that poor crazy old Jenkins, who kept up the fires over at Tater Hill School, for years before they finally sent him to the nutty house at Evansville. Then her sayin' she's *particular,* like she does — expectin' us all to believe her."

"All I can say is that Cosey had better be glad she's got a job," Mary Goss Miller said as she rolled up the tablecloth. "Men are finding jobs hard to come by, so Cosey would be better off to let the men alone. My Paul says he's going to write to the President about finding him a job. All Paul knows is coal-mining, and I've told him that writing won't do him no good. Things look pretty black everywheres."

Jakeyville got it first glimpse of Mr. Sappington at the P.T.A. meeting in September. After Mr. Lamprey introduced him, Sappington called Mrs. Sappington up out of the audience to introduce her. Later the fawners surged forward to introduce themselves in an attempt to impress Mr. Sappington with their own importance, to work for favors for their own offspring, and to re-emphasize their certainty that each parent's child was a genius who needed only a slight advantage over these others to prove his unusual capacities.

Cosey halfheartedly joined in the scramble. But when Mr. Sappington shook off his crowd of fawners and came obediently to his wife's side, Cosey preened herself to attention with an age-old gleam in her eye. From her own experience she had decided that a man who showed his wife so much attention before a crowd must have something guilty — perhaps he had been caught many times — to hide.

The attraction of Cosey for the ever-so-formal Sappington gave Jakeyville something else to laugh over; at the same time it provided Cosey with something to talk about. Which she did.

✻

Miller's Woods was quiet that day, for many of Jakeyville's residents were glued to radio receivers. Lindbergh was making a speech; his many flights were the talk of the year. Mr. Noah Cloud, the scoutmaster, excused himself from the duties of chaperon for a planned hike in order to listen. "Why, one of these days we'll be flyin' them things just like they was automobiles!" Noah declared in an effort to impress the small fry. The boys could not let history interrupt their trip to Miller's Woods, where the Shakamak enticed them with its banks sentineled by cattails, and Eden Swamp was a dare to the bravest, to gather specimens of wild life. (At least that is what they later told Noah Cloud.)

Four of the most venturesome boys, Jay Miller, Red Poe, Whitey Slack, and George Dillen Hawroth, separated themselves by intention from the rest of the group. Red Poe carried the bucket in which they planned to transport the frog they were after to Cosey's mailbox, or, if they dared, to her desk at school.

"Best place for frogs is there by Moses' Rock," George said. "Best time's at night." He rolled the gunny sack firmly to tuck it inside his leather belt around the waist of his overalls. "Catchin' just one frog should be easy."

"Easier than snipe-huntin'," Jay retaliated, for he, the youngest, had been the latest victim of the joke played on smaller boys.

The path emerged into a clearing where the sun made an unexpected bright puddle of light to defy the heavy surrounding foliage of the deep woods. Here, it seemed, Arachne and Minerva competed to weave the pattern of the looms so that the charmed nymphs would be attracted.

"We'll have to keep real quiet from here on in, or frogs'll hear us comin' and head for Davy Jones's locker," George, as oldest of the group, warned. "You go first on the path, Jay. Red next, then Whitey. I'll follow with the sack."

The hanging vines were heavy with the moisture of the recent rains. On each side of the narrow path, which trailed through the treacherous marshes, Jack-in-the-pulpits delivered lectures which fell on the listening green ears of the violet plants and over the broad backs of the may-apple leaves. The perfume from the wild honeysuckle struggled, as good struggles always to outreach the evil, represented by the three-leaved, red-dusted poison ivy fronds, to change the face of Life itself. Fallen dead logs tried to get into the all-living act by acquiring a part-camouflage of bright green moss, much as a woman uses bright colors to draw attention away from fading flesh paled by Time's decay; for in every new and living thing Death's nearness is ever present. Why do we run from it as fast as hope can carry us? For when the years weigh down the hands of our clock, as rust has long weighed down the hands of the clock in the Genesis County Courthouse, we will look for the secret of youth everlasting — search for it diligently — and it will remain a hidden secret, lost forever in the passage of time.

George Dillen Hawroth, at the rear of the procession, chewed on a sassafras stem. In a guarded whisper, a strange habit of those who walk in a woods, he confided his secret wish to Whitey.

"As many times as I have come hunting through these woods, and as many times as I've heard it told how the Genesis Trees all died out hereabouts, I just keep looking, hoping that I'll discover one. Uncle Pete's told that they brought the first Genesis Tree into the Territory from Asia. A religious sect down at New Harmony called it a Raintree and planted it in their 'Athens of the West.' A shame they died out."

"Do you really think they died out natural-like, or do you think it was a curse?" Jay asked.

"You and those curses, Jay," teased Red. "Think the devil himself is hidin' behind any of these trees?"

"Who knows. I don't make fun of nothin' since the teacher read that story about that horseman riding in the woods with his head in his hands, believe you me!"

"Aw, that's a fairy story some guy made up. Now for me I'll take my blarney with some of them tales out of *Smokehouse Monthly,*" Red volunteered.

"Your mom would blister you if she found you readin' one. My dad brought one home once, and Mom threatened to throw him out with it. I looked it over while they were fightin', and all I could see was a poem about Frankie and Johnny — not bad at all. She just shot him, that's all."

The path narrowed between some berry bushes through which

the boys stepped gingerly. Snakes were respected even in Genesis County.

"Betcha I wouldn't be afraid of any snake, 'less it was a rattler. Dad says he used to see 'em near this swamp. Used to catch 'em, too."

"Kinda funny, ain't it, how everybody's scared of snakes. Outside of the poison kind, they ain't really so harmful," Red explained.

"Just the same I'll miss 'em every chance I get," George admitted.

"Betcha wouldn't if one was settin' on a limb of one of them Genesis Trees you're always lookin' for."

"Well," George grinned, "that case would be different. You guys just laugh all you want to, but I'll bet if I ever found one I'd find out what the secret is about how they came here. They say they can't be started from seeds. Must be a good reason," George explained. "That's why someday, when I've solved the mystery about the Genesis Tree, and maybe the secret of what Life is all about, I'll share it with others. That way everyone on earth would be happy, just as God intended for Adam and Eve to be."

George stopped to pick a Jack-in-the-pulpit, flipped "Jack" with his finger, looked to see in which way Jack leaned, and decided his fortune — in the direction Jack leaned. Then, as was the custom, he tossed the plant away.

"George, what do you suppose *is* the answer to the riddle of Life? What really is *good,* and what really is *evil?* If the Genesis Tree could give the answer, don't you think your people, or even God Himself, would have kept one alive?"

"Who knows? Even my Uncle Pete, the Fiddlin' Man, doesn't know. But the Genesis Tree is so involved in the history of my people that I just keep on looking for one. It would be like finding a part of me that once was, a sort of link-like with my kin folks. I've looked everywhere, I guess. Uncle Pete says if there's ever a place where one still grows, it would be here where Eden Swamp joins in near Shakamak."

"You know why it got the name of Eden?" Whitey asked.

" 'Cause it's such a famous smootchin' place for — "

"Shu-ussh!" Jay signaled by holding out his arms at the front of the procession down the hill. "If that ain't Eve in the Garden of Eden, I'll scratch my —"

"Eve?" Red sputtered as he felt a blush of forbidden guilt flood up from the neck of his blue-denim shirt. "M-my eye!" The sun through the trees made his hair look redder as he stretched his neck until he leaned on Jay's shoulder. The scene below them was in direct focus. "Th-that's Miss Cosey. And her half nekkid, sure as shootin'!"

As the four boys watched from shelter, Cosey Walters hung her shapeless summer voile dress on a nearby limb. Then, with her white chemise half covering her stayed corset, she sat down on a rock to remove her beige shoes and stockings. She glanced at her watch, with its black ribbon band, on her wrist before removing it. The boys feared discovery as she glanced over her shoulder in their direction. As one they gasped when Cosey, certain that she was alone, stepped, in an imitation of daintiness, into the edge of the water. She seemed to shake all over as one toe tested the chilled water. Again she looked up the hill in the direction of the boys' hiding place.

The quartet remained as quiet as a quail on eggs; each felt his throat muscles suck at the Adam's-apple in disbelief. Their parents spoke of Cosey with respect; yet none of the boys had missed the knowing laughter parents attached to Cosey's unsuccessful romantic pursuits. *What was Cosey doing here alone in Eden Swamp?*

Their time of wonder was cut short. A snapping twig, on the path on the hill above and in back of them, betrayed the presence of another human being.

"It's Super-in-tend-ent Sappington," George groaned. "He's acoming our way. We're trapped!"

"What-what'll we do?" Red moaned. "He'll catch us watchin' sure. Be our necks!" Red had felt often the sting of Sappington's paddle on his bare palms at various times during the past school year.

"Just act like we had a right t-to b-be here," Jay bluffed. "Our right's good as their'n. Free country, you know?"

Daniel faced the lions with more courage than these frightened boys could muster up. Could the strict, unsmiling Mr. Sappington hear their hearts hammering like woodpeckers on a pine tree? If they ran, Cosey would guess they had been watching her partial-stripping for her private wading. Fear spread to dampen the white skin on the backs of their denim-covered legs. If Cosey and Sappington were holding a planned rendezvous, the matter was even worse. But how could they warn him to halt without Cosey being warned also by the sound of their voices? Charybdis smiled on as Scylla beckoned, and God searched the garden for Adam and Eve.

... Is there a misery of indecision that haunts the joy of being a youth? Or did a vengeful god challenge with: *What creature is this in the morning of its life* ... ?

All of the boys were in agony while George squirmed as though he had a pocketful of mice. As their recognized leader, they awaited his decision. "Can you make it up a tree?" George asked heavyweight Whitey.

"I-I-I — " Whitey could find no such capable tree close by. His momentary pause proved to be their undoing. Mr. Sappington's bulk was framed abruptly by heavy foilage above them on the path.

"Ahem," he challenged, taking advantage of his surprise. From his hip pocket he pulled a huge white handkerchief to swipe at the shiny perspiration on his broad forehead, and then at his neck which bulged about the line of his tight collar. "And what are you boys doing in Eden Swamp today? Didn't Noah Cloud make arrangements for you to hear Lindbergh?"

The blushing boys, roasting from the burn of embarrassment much hotter than the sun, couldn't answer.

The flustered superintendent pressed his slight advantage, an old trick of the guilty. "Why is it we educators, who work so hard to give you the advantages of education, cannot obtain the cooperation of you pupils? Think how boys in foreign countries would appreciate opportunities! You boys prefer to wander in the wilderness, and to refuse the floods of manna that are raining from heaven at this very moment."

Red found his tongue to ask as he peered innocently up at the sun. "Is it really raining manna?"

"Not literally, you — " He raised his arms in his excitement to free the folded copy of *Indianapolis Views* tucked under his arm. "Why aren't you listening to Lindbergh?" He stepped forward to catch Red's arm.

Self-preservation made Red blurt before he thought, "Wh-why aren't you?"

"Why I, why I . . ." Mr. Sappington was a huge fresh ham being barbecued in front of the hungry crowd at the annual Miners' Picnic. *Supposing these boys had seen Cosey? Supposing they had been waiting here a while just to trap him?* Never again could he get a job as superintendent; the flood of gossip would seek him out everywhere. *Oh, for the raven of Noah; oh for the dove!* DOVE? Wasn't a dove a symbol of peace? He knew, as he swallowed hard, that he had no choice but to retreat to save his face. Peace, *that was it!* Switching to olive-branch psychology, he tried to coax his face back to its normal shade of red.

George Dillen Hawroth picked up the dropped newspaper and extended it courteously to the superintendent.

"Thank you, my boy," said Sappington as he placed the paper once again under his arm. *Wasn't this the same voice Jacob used to fool Isaac?* Fumbling about for a place to begin, his eyes fell upon the newspaper. "Now that's a fine question: What was I doing here?" He complimented Red. "I was cutting through Eden Swamp to take this copy of Lindbergh's speech so that she could read it to you in class. Yes, that's just what I was doing. Exactly, ahem." He cleared his throat, and was so pleased that he could find a lie that he celebrated by running his thumb up and down his galluses. "But I suppose you boys were gathering specimens for scouting?" He fished for information.

"Yep. I mean, yes, sir," Whitey volunteered, glad for a way out.

"Then you are indeed in luck. Being alert, as are all of we who have been called to serve in this scant-rewarding profession of educating, I noticed a strange tree growing at the edge of the swamp just east of here, near Nod's farm. I have never before seen leaves like those on this young tree." He tried to conjure up a clumsy attempt at humor. "So go East, young men, go east of Eden and make a discovery for yourselves. You can bring the fruit of the tree to Miss Cosey's Nature Study Class on Monday, and ask her to — "

"Oh, we wouldn't have to wait until Monday," Whitey interrupted in his efforts to quickly talk the boys out of an embarrassing spot. "Miss Cosey's — ugh!"

The toe of Jay Miller's shoe caught Whitey in the small of his back. With no time to close his mouth, Whitey was pitched violently forward. George and Jay sprang over to pick him up and to silence him with warning looks as they brushed off the sputtering Whitey.

"We'll leave right away, sir," George chattered to fill in for Jay's unexplained action. "We're going to take your advice right now. Yes, we are. You can bet we are." He breathed a sigh of relief at their narrow escape.

Fate was against Cosey that day. The boys had put a distance of fifty feet between them and Sappington when a water moccasin chose that moment to slither into the water. Cosey's scream of fright pierced the damp-woods silence like a scolding jay.

A serpent was once again proving to be the undoer of a woman in Eden.

George Dillen Hawroth did not dare to turn around as the boys ran from the scene. From the corner of his eye, George glimpsed the frustrated Sappington as the heavy man trundled down the hill — an accomplishment George might have otherwise believed impossible had he not seen it — to Cosey's aid.

When he and the boys were safely over the ridge and out of sight, George dropped to his knees to roll, convulsed with laughter, with the others on the turf. "It was merely a coincidence, purely a meeting of two great educator's minds in the cause of science."

As they watched from the concealment of bushes, Superintendent

Sappington, in less than five minutes, emerged at the top of the crest. He looked carefully to his right and to his left before leaving Miller's Woods to return to town. His folded newspaper was still under his arm.

"You reckon Cosey's okay?" Red asked, for the boys felt a genuine affection for their teacher.

"Guess so," George answered. "But you and your big mouth. You almost told him we had seen Cosey."

Whitey's grin was as guilty as a boy with matches in a closet before Christmas. "I was eager to agree with him so that we could get away. It just slipped out before I thought. What do you s'pose he'll say to us when he sees us now?"

"What can he say?" George answered. "What can one say at such a time? For Cosey's sake, let's give them the benefit of the doubt, call it a coincidence."

"But what if we see something like this happen again?" Jay puzzled.

"If?" George asked. "Well, it wouldn't be the first time it's happened in Indiana's woods, nor will it be the last time. Lots of customs had their beginning right here in Genesis County, but Nature's garden has been a trysting place since Creation's morning."

"Sure," Red agreed. "So let's head for home. We've had enough excitement for one day."

As the boys moved away, George hesitated. "Tell you what. You guys go on. Me, I'm going to take a look-see at that tree Sappington mentioned."

"Oh, you! Always lookin' for that Genesis Tree," Red teased. "My dad says they died out in this part of Indiana long ago."

"I know," George agreed. "But water's been low this spring. Just might be such a thing that a seed, planted long ago, might find earth that suits it and decide to grow. Golly, what I'd give just to find one, thorns, thistles and all. Maybe it would solve our riddles about a lot of things!"

"Oh, for forty years of wandering in the wilderness," Whitey called back as the other boys left George. "You and your secret riddles. You may end up another Johnny Appleseed like your Uncle Pete tells about coming through Indiana. But let us know if you make a startling discovery; we'll share and share alike."

"Yeah, maybe you'll find buried treasure, too, like in the legend," Red teased. "If you could really discover the Tree of Life, we'd all be rich with the treasure."

"I'm not looking for treasure, exactly — unless you count knowledge as treasure," George defended. "I'll be satisfied if I find out just a little of what this life's all about — solve the riddle, maybe, right here in Genesis County."

And when the others were gone, George Dillen Hawroth went eastward from Eden Swamp. He looked down as his hands and, lo, they were the hands of another searcher of Genesis County.

> *. . . And the Lord God commanded the man, saying, Of every tree of the garden thou mayest freely eat: But of the tree of the knowledge of good and evil, thou shalt not eat of it; for in the day that thou eatest thereof thou shalt surely die.*

. . . Why did God choose to leave women out when He said, *"It is not good that the man should be alone,"* Cosey Walters puzzled. "Why did he slight me without a helpmeet? I'm more'n willin' to help meet a decent man more'n halfway . . ."

Cosey had relived the scene, or had planned it in her mind, of her chance meeting with Superintendent Sappington many times. How she longed to make that picture on the cover of the book of Myths, that one of Aphrodite, spring to life! In dreams only could the role of heroine be hers.

Yet isn't it better to cherish a dream than to settle for nothing? "It must be," she told her reflection in the mirror one day while using tortoise-shell hairpins to secure the bundle of her hair at the nape of her neck. "Maybe God compensates us, the have-nots, by permitting us to keep our precious thoughts from others."

There in the wool-rug, shade-drawn darkness of her parlor, Cosey's nervous laugh was as alum on a cut. What would the pupils, their parents, or Mr. Sappington think if they could hear her talking to herself? Most of all, what would Mr. Sappington (did she dare call him Adam in her dreams?) think? Could he, could anyone, know how melancholy are the sounds of loneliness? There have always been lonely people, the forgotten ones who hide away from those who are too busy to care. But the truly lonely, Cosey knew from experience, are those who try to hide loneliness by secreting it from unsympathetic eyes, and those who use pretense to plug up the hole in the dike. The graveyards in Genesis County kept the secret of the number of those drowned, the victims of the searching, in the ever pounding floods of Loneliness.

Cosey sped dutifully out into the plant room on her house; there in the bay window was her family, the rows of African violet plants. Each flower-child tilted his purple velvet face for a drink, to be admired, and to be cuddled by mothering fingertips while demanding its "formula" of feeding to keep it growing. To Cosey, signs of wilt brought alarm, the same alarm which threatens the mother who discovers a child with a fevered brow; for these were Cosey's children, and all the earthly descendents she would ever have.

Cosey made a minute inspection of her flower-children before she left that day. Could the violets guess that her heart was missing beats owing to the excitement of contemplated wickedness?

As she made her way toward Miller's Woods, gingerly threading in and out of weed growths to preserve her beige-colored lisle stockings, she rehearsed her plan. Mr. Sappington (Adam?) told her he was going to bring "something of importance" to her school on the other side of Miller's Woods. If she would tell him that, quite by chance, her watch had stopped on her way to the school, so that time just got away while she was wading, he would not think that coming upon the scene would be unusual. If Adam could only see her as Aphrodite, as a woman away from the schoolroom, maybe . . .

And hadn't he said expressly, "I'll be coming by way of Eden

Swamp, you know, along the Shakamak path. I love nature, and . . ."

Need he have extended a more pointed invitation? thought Cosey. *I'll teach them — Bella, Trixie, Mary and the rest to laugh behind my back!* The old bitterness returned.

With all in readiness, with the entry scene and all of the visualized results it might bring mentally recounted inside Cosey's secret mind for the hundredth time, the water moccasin appeared in the shallow water. The consequences, her scream, jarred her so that in her haste to reach the bank she fell. The muddy water connived with the devil. She stood up looking more like a barrel than Aphrodite with her clothing clinging to her, drenched with mud. Half of her dark hair masked her face like a beard; the rest clung like a horse's wet tail to her back. Water-lily leaves and moss slime clung to her bare arms and legs. A minnow plopped from her bosom back to lake-safety just as Mr. Sappington awkwardly extended his hand.

"May I be of some service?" he said before backing away, quite discreetly, to where the bank rose behind him.

"A serpent," Cosey tried to explain as she crossed her hands across her chest. "A s-serpent," she sputtered as she moved toward the concealment of a rock.

The hollow sound of snapping twigs announced the quick departure of Mr. Sappington.

Why is it that no words have been written for the music of interruption? Even the darers, those who wish to offer love on an impermanent basis, are imprisoned by the moral code and wear around their necks the keys to their own cells. Like Cosey, they know it is an investment in inner security they cannot spend. There is the clash of sounding brass upon tinkling cymbals, and the symphony of unrequited love becomes the theme song of life for the lover, a complaining melody.

She would have to wait now for her clothes to dry. In the places of savage light she would lift her head and say she didn't care. Memory would return her often to this scene, the secret place in the earth, the paradise, the Delphic Caves . . .

PART FOUR

Stubby Wakefield

The devil, they say, ran plum out of space
In hell with the furnace roar.
He looked all over the whole damn place
And couldn't find room for more.

But a company boss who lived there then
Advised him to look again;
When Satan discovered Old Number Nine Pit,
That's where he sent the men.

"Go dig that coal from the endless night!
You'll rue the day of your birth!"
So the dead men fastened their chains again
To descend to hell below earth.

And when they were hid from Satan's sight,
They laughed till the rats squealed high.
"We've worked in Hell most of our life;
At last we are learning why."

STUBBY WAKEFIELD

HAD PARVIN WAKEFIELD known that first day, when at thirteen he traded his school books for a pick with which to follow his father down into the deep mines, that a slate fall, later on, would brand him with the name "Stubby" for the rest of his life, he might have run away north as some others did. Not knowing, Parvin accepted Pa's decision as his duty to help earn money needed at home. With so many mouths to feed, Pa's dollar a day for ten hours' work didn't go very far at the company-owned store.

In the two-room shanty, Parvin stretched out on his pallet on the kitchen floor and pretended to sleep as his parents discussed his fate while facing each other across the round table. A kerosene lamp, sputtering to be heard, danced meaningful shadows on the faded walls of the room. The dim light was kind to his mother's drawn face; it kept the deep lines webbed there by childbirth's pain, anxiety, and want a secret.

"I wanted Parvin to get learnin', so's he wouldn't be a miner," Ma objected timidly. "Hain't we lost enough menfolks to the mines now? Even my own pa and brother."

"My grandpa was loadin' coal when he was eight," Pa bragged, his tone warning her to quit championing education's cause. "He could read and write, too. Minin' — workin' with his hands — never hurt him none."

Ma looked down at her own callused hands, red from lye soap and winter's chaff. Ashamed, she thrust them under her apron.

"Workin' with the hands never hurt no one," Ma agreed. "Bible says so. Yet I hoped Parvin would get to stick to schoolin'." Mother's instinct to protect the young made her bolder. "And then there's always so much trouble in the mines."

"Labor trouble, you mean? Why, it's to be expected. My people had it in the old country afore they come here. Sure there's trouble now and then. That's why we have the Committee. Right now the I.W.W. stewin' 'cause they're gettin' too big for their britches. Meant to make the unions stronger, they're brewin' riots, forcin' out the state militia. Gene Debs didn't plan on these hotheads takin' over."

"Just the same, if this troublemakin' I.W.W. gets control of the mines, they'll tear down all the miners it built up. Debs is too honest to stick with that I.W.W. He'd make a good President, too. But they'll never let a workin' man get elected."

Pa reached across the table to adjust the lamp, only because the odor and soot made his eyes smart. "Miners need better wages, better conditions. But until someday comes, we'll need what Parvin can make to feed the rest of us."

Somewhere from the other room a hungry baby cried, restless in its sleep. Ma hurried to it while agreeing, by her silence, to fix Parvin's bucket in the morning.

Parvin did not betray pain at their decision by movement. For him a new life was beginning before his life in the schoolroom had finished. The room, the pot-bellied stove, the cracked blackboard, and Teacher Potter's stiff mustache all seemed suddenly dear. The brown feist dog who waited outside for him, day after day, would wait no more. One tear squeezed out from under his eyelid and rolled down his cheek. The younger Wakefields, Parvin knew, would quarrel over their inheritance — the precious tablet and penny pencil — he abandoned forever in favor of a shovel and an even chance at survival in the starless arena of danger.

At four the next morning in 1912, Ma woke him up. Parvin, who had gone to sleep a boy, was now a man, a man entitled to a working man's breakfast.

Ma busied herself over the smoking cookstove when they left, just as if she couldn't stand the sight of her firstborn leaving to enter the mines.

In a topless buggy, their legs wrapped against the chilling

December morning in old patch quilts, Parvin rode beside Pa down the mud-crusted road the two miles to the highway. Parvin watched steam from the horse's nostrils puff and disappear under a sky promising dawn.

An hour later, at the mine, they hurried to unhitch the horse, feed, and change clothes to go below. At 7 A.M. the cars, loaded with lamp-capped miners, descended. Miners who were late had to enter the mine by a "manway," a series of short stairways that wound their way down almost three hundred feet to the bottom of Dan Webster Mine.

From a company-owned supply shack Pa charged, to the number assigned to Parvin, a pair of canvas pants, a cap, and a miner's lamp. The rubber shoes issued, to be worn without socks, laced halfway up to Parvin's knees. No warm shelter was provided in which to change clothes. Other miners seemed to ignore, with kindness, his nudeness; but the December chill cut into Parvin's skinny, naked shoulders like salt into a fishhook wound.

"Bite down hard to keep your teeth from chattering," Pa ordered the shaking boy with blue lips. "Want them other d——groundhogs to think you're a whale-whimperer? Follow me."

With only an outgrown frayed sweater to protect his bare shoulders, Parvin joined the other men on the descending cage. A heavy chain, head high, boxed in the four by six feet platform.

"Grab on to the chain, Parvin. Hold on! It's better if you close your eyes."

At a speed controlled by steam pressure, much faster than gravity, the cage descended. At the bottom Parvin couldn't wait the unloading before his breakfast, forced up into his mouth, shot out of him.

It was a while after that before his eyes became accustomed to the dark where miners' dim lamps seemed suspended in space about him. He heard them talking, bantering each other as they moved about, long before their ghostly faces swam into focus.

"Hope that groundhog of your'n's got web toes, too," the other miners kidded Pa. "Looks like we'll swim with shovels today," they joked. "Can you swim, Parvin? Your pa here's a good un."

After Pa cut twine string for a lamp wick, Parvin placed the cap on his head and followed Pa down a tunnel to their left. At first they walked upright. The tunnel seemed to get lower as they advanced until, after a hundred feet, they were bent over almost double.

Another two hundred feet, they stopped at a point where the tunnel narrowed to about twelve feet wide. The walls were ebony. Water dripped at intervals so that the track used by the cars was in places submerged. Heavy stones, looking as if they would come crashing down at any moment, hung precariously from the roof. In places heavy oak logs helped prop up the roof.

A roaring rumble warned them. Pa grabbed his arm to shout.

"The coal car's comin' this way toward the cage shaft at the Main Entry. There's a trip comin' out. Get off the track and stand by one of them props over there!"

As the fearsome roaring came closer, Parvin could hear the four mules, hitched in single file with leather shields on their heads to protect them against bumping the low ceiling, pulling the loaded cars and rattling their harness chains. The driver, hunched like a turtle with a bull's neck, flashed his long whip to sting the sweating mules along their ribs as they pulled by.

The tiny creatures dragged thirty tons. When the driver took his hand from the rump of the mule directly in front of him to uncoil the blacksnake whip from around his neck, the coming terror warned the animals. Their eyes bulged as the whip cut flesh and the driver hurled vile oaths to urge them on to more speed.

Parvin felt his thin chest convulse as he sobbed in sympathy for the driven, enduring animals. *Like me,* he thought as he knew their fate was not unlike his own. "Never, never," he murmured under his breath, "will I be a mule driver." The heavy stench stirred up by the mule sweat and their waste on the track made his eyes sting with fire.

A piercing squeak, coming from beneath his feet, startled him as he stumbled, half sick from witnessing the brutality to mules, in the wet, mucky darkness. "Wh-what's th-hat?" he managed to ask.

"Only a rat. A big one. See?" Pa pointed at a huge pair that waited, only five feet away, their whiskers waving in curiosity. "We feed 'em. 'S what makes 'em so big. They're our luck . . . warn us when there's a crack up above, or the slate's saggin'."

"And wh-what," he asked his father as they squatted there to begin picking coal from the solid wall which faced them, "what do you do if there's a slate fall comin'?"

"You run. When the rats leave, son, drop everythin' and run like hell for the cage. Them rats knows. Only God knows how they knows. But no miner from Genesis County or anywheres else will return to the working face when the rats leave. Don't you dare harm one of 'em, understand. Without 'em and the canaries they carry in to warn of gas in the tunnel, few of us would live to see daylight again."

"But can't they pump this water out, Pa, so's it won't be so cold?" he asked.

"Sure, but without the water, dust forms. Our lamps ignite it so it explodes. Wouldn't be enough left of us to scrape off the walls. You'll get plenty warm once we start loadin' cars," he promised.

That first week Parvin learned why the mines claim only the young to chain to the smell, the midnight-forever, and the damp. A man will not voluntarily enter a mine when he is grown. A child learns early to accept the danger; after a while he is too ashamed to admit he is afraid. So the miners must beget miners to replace themselves.

Weeks later Parvin could take a ribbing as well as any of the older men. A miner had to learn to take it if he shared the air they all breathed; dust and damp and White Death made them all of one family.

And what made them of one body? Was it their black hides, greased for warmth as they worked, naked to the waist in the icy knee-high miniature ponds which flooded the pits?

Parvin felt the tremor as the fan, bringing February-fresh air from the shaft, pumped new life into the entry. The sting of it bit his skinny ribs. He shivered. His shovel often trembled in his hands, but not from the chill, reassuring wind seeping into the face of the coal. His shovel trembled in his blistered hands for the same reason all miners' shovels trembled in secret — the trembling that made them all of one body: FEAR!

. . . and of such is the Kingdom of Fear. And to thee we give the praise, the honor, and the *gory* . . .

THE GORY OF HONOR

They said that they drank to kill fear. As almost all miners drank, the saloons were full on weekday nights. On payday and Saturday nights they overflowed.

Most of the fights in Genesis County, some leading to killings, flourished on payday nights.

The quarrels began deep in the mines for two reasons. One was a bread-and-butter situation. When a man loaded a car to be sent to the screeners for weighing he tagged it with a metal disk bearing his assigned number. Coal is loosened by a blasting shot; some is released in lumps, the rest in fine slack which slips through the screen when weighed. Thus, a man loading all slack received no pay at all. If a miner, who must keep his entry clean of all coal, was forced by assignment from a boss to load more than his fair share of slack, he was being cheated. Rivalry over choice assignments was keen — a bone of contention meaning FIGHT.

The second quarrel breeder was women. No matter what foreign accent a miner's speech betrayed, he was a blood brother to the offended when it came to protecting a feminine relative's good name.

A *woman-fight* did not need a bottle's contents to fire it into action, nor did they wait for the saloon's larger space to begin. The mule drivers, men who seemed to hold a nameless kind of brutality within themselves, were worse about this than any other group. The mule drivers kept apart and did not mix with the diggers above or below the surface of Genesis County; their black-snake whips seemed to be the badge with which mule drivers held together this strange fraternity. Together they always sat in a group, separating themselves, while miners congregated near a main entry for the thirty-minute lunch period.

Parvin saw a private fight fester one day as the mule drivers sat in a circle, their black fingers making smudges on their white-bread sandwiches. Women they had known or coveted were, as usual, their favorite subject. World War I was a fever-pitch and the war-time dip of morals was being felt even on the home front.

"Got me a gal in Clinton who's glad to be waiting," Seppia, the broad, squat Italian driver bragged. "She's a hotel job, she is. To everyone else she's as strict as a Sunday school teacher. But with David Seppia, this Peggy Sharm's a — "

Seppia never finished the sentence. A huge hairy-handed man, known only as "Irish," leaped from the circle to knock Seppia over backwards. With his right hand Irish uncoiled the black-snake whip from around his neck and began to beat the cowering Seppia, who howled in pain.

The same pity which Parvin felt that day when the mules were whipped squeezed him now.

This time the milk of pity was watered with disgust. He could feel tears heating his coal-dusted eyelids. "Run!" reason argued. Yet Parvin was glued to the spot, fascinated by the drama one animal was enacting upon another. Blood from whipcuts striped down Seppia's back as he screamed for mercy. Why didn't the other drivers interfere? They were bound by their code of silence, where justice over womenfolk is a man's own personal privilege. Backing away, the other drivers offered Irish the unspoken courtesy of lots of room.

Parvin could not move back. Suddenly, as he stood hypnotized, he felt his lunch of salt pork and apple being retched up. He clasped his arms over his stomach and leaned forward. As he did, the razor-sharp end of Irish's whip caught him across the neck and throat. He pitched forward on his face as he felt blood leave his brain. Mercifully, he fainted . . .

Minutes later, miner friends of Pa's helped to revive Parvin.

"You stopped the floggin'," one called Li'l Texas offered. "Irish said to tell you he's sorry you got in the way. You won't bleed long."

Parvin struggled to his feet as another asked: "Feel like going back to your entry?"

"Guess so," Parvin managed to reply as his fingertips gingerly tested the burning edges of the cut. Blood had dripped into a small oil-puddle on the coal floor. "Wh-what happened to Seppia?"

"Don't waste no feelin' on him, Parvin. The sonovabitch got what was comin'. He's left Dan Webster, turned in his number. Won't dare work at Dan Webster no more. But let that be a lesson to you when you're older. Chase all the women you've a mind to, but keep your d—— face shut about it. Might never know whose sister she might'n be."

On hair-spring legs Parvin walked toward his entry. A piercing squeal caused him to look back over his shoulder. A huge rat was drinking at the spilled human blood, his whiskers red and weaving at his feast.

Oh what's the difference? Parvin decided as he hurried away. *Man* or *rat. All the same* . . .

The whip's cut would leave a scar because coal dust, ground in, would help mark it, he knew. The red bandanna he would have to wear around his neck to hide it would become his badge of courage. Would his ugly scar become the *mark of the beast* Ma read about in the Bible? Or would it be the mark of Cain that would someday, like Cain's, cause him to repeat Cain's violence — to take the life of a close kin? . . .

Either way the scar didn't matter; it would serve its purpose in planting the seed of brutality inside a frightened boy. The mine-bred learned fear; the fear-bred learned hate; the hate-bred learned to fight back. And how does one fight back? By the only way one knows, taught by those around him. *Make others feel the pain balling up inside you. Make them suffer, too!* And maybe, by some quirk of twisted reasoning, it will lessen the all-consuming fear that drives all of us on toward death . . .

"And dear God," Parvin prayed quietly because he felt God

couldn't hear from these damp depths anyhow. "When it comes — when it comes to me — don't let it be down here. Don't let it be down here where no one'll know . . . where no one'll care . . ."

His child-years' term as Fear's prisoner was faithfully counted. Hoping for parole, Parvin told himself that times would change, that new and better prisons would be built, and that he would eventually be freed. The Warden of Darkness laughed at Parvin's hope till the walls of coal, the face, the roof, and the bottom nearly split at their seams. The Warden's best deputies, Crippler and Death, laughed with him; they knew a lifer when they got one, knew that Parvin would have to come to one or both of them to escape Fear's prison — if he ever did. *We got his brother with Black Damp, didn't we . . . ?*

The first set of gates swung closed without Parvin's knowledge. While standing in a line with other men who awaited the counting of their steel tags, taken during the past week from the cars each man had loaded, to be multiplied out into pay-gold, Pa broached the subject of Parvin's future.

"When you're twenty-one, you're free to keep your own earnin's. You'll be marryin' up with some gal one of these nights . . . need it. Joe's comin' up fourteen soon. Old Enoch's promised to start Joe as trip boy over at the Queen."

Memory of his own sentence ignited an injustice still fresh in Parvin's mind. Because the owners of Hamilton Mine had refused to let the miners adopt the improved carbide lamps — they contended that the old-style lamps would go out in the presence of Black Damp to warn the miners — the protesting miners had come out on a long strike. The Hamilton was idle for a great while, long enough for damp which had collected on the bottom to claim the life of Benj, Parvin's younger brother.

"No," Parvin disagreed with Pa, and tremblingly held his ground. "The mine got Benjamin, only sixteen. We're goin' to let Joe finish school."

Pa stepped from the line, turned to face Parvin, and threatened, his fist uplifted. "Hold your tongue. Never reared no young'n to be a schoolin' loafer, too good for minin'. Nor a sasser neither."

The coal-blackened men, with eyes shining like white marbles, turned as one to watch. Each hoped to see a fight — to relieve monotony.

Pa lowered his voice as the line of miners fanned out; the men yearned for a rare father-son fight to begin. "You'll be wantin' money of your own soon. My buddy told me he seen you and Jacob Letszinger hanging around outside the prayer meetin' two weeks on a straight. Want to tell your pa who the frill is?" He nudged toward Parvin's ribs playfully with his elbow. The watchers, although disappointed that a fight was not ensuing, roared with coarse laughter. What is this joke so secret that I cannot understand? Parvin asked himself.

From the pattern fashioned by the old-country traditions brought from homelands by the miners, Parvin was allowed at twenty-one to keep his wages for the first time. Weeks later he married Sarah Fields Wilson, a beauty who was going on sixteen, and rented an unpainted shack, one of the many company-owned block houses in the Dan Webster Blocks. With his solemn wedding vows he promised himself to save his money for the purpose of moving north later on, away from the mines — to a hill farm, maybe.

Sarah celebrated her twenty-first birthday by giving birth to their fourth child, a second son, Peter. Their first son, Abram, was four; Rebecca was three. Their third child, Lizzie, who had lived a few weeks, was buried out on the hill in the company-owned graveyard.

When Lizzie died, Parvin's strange behavior had shocked Sarah.

"You're not goin' to work with Lizzie layin' here in her coffin, are you?" Sarah protested that night in the kitchenroom. Weak from her latest ordeal of childbirth, she leaned across the cookstove to rest her head on the warming oven for support.

"Might as well," Parvin answered defiantly, wanting to hurt her.

Sarah was puzzled. Why did this outward cruelty seem his only way of building up a bluff against his growing fear of dying inside a deep mine? She had watched it spring up like ragweed from the dusty heat along the shale road at Nod's Crossing, where it had choked out all other growth. Would Parvin never escape this fear? Would it grow like the ruby scar the whip had cut at his throat — a scar like the mark of Cain?

The heat from the cookstove brought a flush to Sarah's face. Parvin felt the urge to comfort her; fighting it, his arms were as wood at his side. Was it a show of weakness for a miner to show pity?

"What's one more brat like L-Lizzie?" he rasped while trying to escape the moment of tenderness. "We'll have plenty more."

"But Granny Freeman, the midwife, said . . . said I shouldn't have any more!" Sarah's cry was from the memory of the long days and nights of piercing pain before Lizzie was delivered.

"You're my woman, ain't you?" Parvin glowered and spat into the coal bucket. He took his cap down from a nail behind the stove. The screen door slammed behind him.

I run things in my shack, he told himself as he swaggered into the night and headed for a saloon in town. A woman ain't no better than a Peabody mule. Has to be beat to know who's boss. To rule with cruelty was the only lie which could hide him. The truth, *he would never be anything but a coal miner,* could no longer be the forest or the trees.

Parvin got very drunk that night. The help of three buddies was required to bring him back to the shack where Sarah waited beside the tiny pine box in the corner. Four neighbor women kept vigil with Sarah. The pies and cakes, brought as neighborly expressions of sympathy, were on the kitchen table, night food for the mourners who were to "sit up" with the dead. Sarah was doubly grateful for the comforting presence of the neighbors; she knew that the fear of being shamed before neighbors would compel Parvin to attend the infant's burial services the next day.

At the graveside Sarah saw him clench his fists, and saw the perspiration of fear bead his forehead as the clods began to fall upon the pine box. Yes, she knew, Parvin's suffering was the greatest of all.

*

Parvin's fear of dying underground grew as the years added muscles, thread upon thread, to his arms and thighs. He longed for courage to break away, to get a job where daylight ruled, where none was afraid, and all men could walk with heads up. Yet the years and added responsibility seemed to forge a stronger chain. More safety precautions were taken by the mine owners as the union's ever increasing strength was felt with the pressure of strikes.

Parvin counted himself lucky those many times he was one of the frightened men who alighted from the cage while the mine whistle screamed the long warning blasts which told the county that an accident had happened deep down in those death-filled passageways.

BLACK DAMP. WHITE DAMP. EXPLOSIONS. SLATE FALLS. The dreaded signal called to the anxious-faced women and children who waited, hovering in groups for warmth, their shawled heads thrust forward like wary turtles. COME GATHER YOUR MAIMED AND DEAD, the whistle ordered. HURRY! TAKE YOUR MAN! TAKE HIM AND SEND US MORE OF YOUR SONS TO TAKE HIS PLACE. A woman never knew, until the grime was wiped away frow a crushed and lifeless form, whether or not it was her man the cage had brought up.

In those early years of marriage Parvin always searched the crowd of women, each impossible to distinguish from the other, as they stood huddled in stony-faced silence. For a while Sarah waited with the loyal. After the time Parvin came home drunk, and threw a cup of hot coffee over her as she rocked Peter, who was screaming with the earache, Sarah no longer waited with the searching, hoping women.

She hopes the next man, the next fall, it'll be me, he told himself with each shovelful of coal he loaded into his car. That would fix her with four livin' and three dead, wouldn't it? He licked his lips, then spat out the black dirt his involuntary action had captured with his tongue. Her and her wantin' me to go to church, reform. Hell, God long ago forgot men who grub out coal. He can't see down this far after He sold us out to the devil . . . even if He cared. From habit, unconsciously formed, he ran his fingers lightly over the whip scar which had branded the mark of Cain upon his throat.

As this great fear — dying underground — drained him of strength, hatred of all things contributing to this consuming fear sprang up to drive him on. From his first job as trip boy, usually the first mine job assigned to the child laborer, Parvin had worked his way up. He now held the lead in the constant competition among the miners for record-weight output per day. Coal produced was weighed after screening; each man was paid according to the number of tons he produced. He enjoyed the envious glances of his "ton men" buddies who good-naturedly told each other: "Follow Parvin down there. Get the boss to assign you to the room next to his. He knows the good veins. Favoritism, that's what it is! We ought to take it up with the jerryman or the union. Get us some coal all lumps, no slack."

As they teased him because he worked so hard to keep his record, Parvin's chest lifted with a pride that rivaled the thrust of the cage as it lifted the mules out in triumph each night. The company did not mourn the loss of a miner by death, for mine labor was plentiful; but the company resented it when miners laid off for a day to attend a miner's funeral.

To lose a mine-broken mule was disaster with a difference; the tragedy often brought the bosses and mine owners scurrying to investigate. The expense of replacing a small, ruby-scarred mule was as rugged as the job of keeping mule drivers.

Mule-driving, although well paid and considered a skill above that of ton men, was a job to be shunned. Day men and jerrymen were hired by the company to keep the rooms from which coal was being drilled and loaded clear of water and debris. A ton-man avoided the assignment of "breaking in" as a mule driver as he dreaded gaseous Black Damp which burned and White Damp which choked.

Parvin's urge to load more coal, to break his own ton record, took him into the new room early that morning. The shot had been "fired in the hole." Smoke was drifting in small puff-sifting clouds as the jerryman loaded the dislodged pieces of loose shale, which vibration had loosened, into an empty cart.

"Don't look so good in here, Parvin," the jerryman assigned to the entry warned. "In the quiet yesterday, when the motors weren't runnin' for an idle day, I could hear the slate fallin' all over. Like a pistol shot it was. Warnin'. I put in some new timbers to support the roof. Better take it easy on this face. Air is slackin' the slate roof. Sing out and clear out if you hear it crackin' overhead!"

"Hold your sermons for them needin' one. There's good clean coal here. Want to bet I break a loadin' record today?"

The jerryman shook his head as he rode his clean-up car to the next room. If a man's a fool, he decided, don't join him just to help him prove he is one. *Don't drive the chariot too near the sun, Apollo warned.*

Parvin ignored the additional warning as his lamp ignited the small gas pockets of Black Damp each time he stretched erect to rest his tiring arms.

The Black Damp gas sounded like the buzzing of bees up against the coal roof, just six feet above the bottom on which he stood. The fall rains had made the earth above the roof heavy with the extra weight of sponged-in water to further encourage the danger of a roof cave-in.

Parvin reached down to retrieve a large lump which had bounced out of the empty car he was loading. In the momentary silence, he heard the echoed cracking of the slate above his head. A warning splitting in the face of the coal directly in front of him followed. He leaned upon his shovel, peering into the mystery of darkness which taunted him, before he resumed the loading of the car. As he moved to his left, a slate-laced chunk of roof, bushel-basket size, fell to his right at the open side of the room.

Driven by fear, Parvin dropped his shovel and lunged in the direction of the passageway. Too late! Truth-agony exploded

inside his brain. "My God." The half-prayer, half-curse tore
from his chest like the roar of Hades' furnace. "My God, don't
let me die in here!"

With a rumble of thunder-sized firecrackers mushrooming up
into cannons, the roof crumbled to catch the lower part of Parvin's body. Chunks from the entry pepperd his head and shoulders,
then rolled away in the dust. Men came running from the other
rooms to his aid, while men in other entries, unaware of the extent
of the danger or how much of the roof would fall as a result of
the break, ran in the direction of the cage which would suck them
up to safety. The mine whistle, as the word spread to the engine
room, began its warning dirge. At the top, the circle of women
with strain-marked faces would be waiting.

Consciousness returned to Parvin at spasmodic intervals. Pain
forced him back into the world of dreams. In this bog-fog world,
he ran like the frightened deer in the Indiana woodland and the
fleeing rabbit with beagle hounds, ears flapping to the bounce of
pursuit, up the corn rows. Mercury's wings were on his feet; the
heavy mine boots were as the down of November's milkpods.

"*Aim for his heel, his Achilles heel!*" the baying hounds shouted
in men's voices. Suddenly the hounds became a herd of squealing,
frightend pigs. COALHOG! The squeal of the wind taunted as he
ran on. Water like cold fall driven rain sprayed his face, then
changed to sting like sleet until his skin blanched from the chill
of it.

A thousand blacksmiths were pulling at his foot. He could
hear in the distance the chant used by the Jackson Hill Mine's
team when it met other mine teams in the annual tug-of-war con-
tests at the Miners' Picnic.

> Hold 'em now. Hold 'em twice. Holy shoutin' Jeso Cry-yst!
> We're bound to win; we're bound to yell.
> Jackson Hill, Jackson Hill, pull like hell!

All the devils in hell were pulling at his left leg . . .
The air sucked into his lungs was warm; it smelled of antiseptic

carbolic acid which made the air as pure as the pure, hot Glendora coal of Sullivan County, and just as gaseous.

The white-starched nurses of Union Hospital in Terre Haute were removing the linseed oil which had been hastily swabbed on by the mine's first-aid team. In the faraway, ghost-like background, huddled together against the wall of the hospital room, his mine buddies conversed in low tones.

". . . Have to pass a paper for Sarah Wakefield in the morning," said one.

"Put me down to donate five tons. No, make it ten," another murmured. Sarah's not got that first dime. With all them young-un's to feed. 'N it looks as iffen it'll be a long stretch . . ."

"He'll walk, the doc says," the third man added. "It'll take time. But he'll sorta drag that left foot — like he'd stubbed it — from now on."

And forever after that, as if the slate fall and exploding Black Damp had been his christening, the name Stubby remained to brand him. Parvin-Stubby's hatred of the name, and how it came to be his, stacked up like a pile of mine timber logs with all his other hates. These hatreds strengthened so that they became a fortress cell inside his Fear's prison. There was no other weapon with which to defend himself, so he worked to strengthen the one he felt was inborn: to be cruel to all living things, men or animals. Brutality emerged to become his mailed fist with which to strike out at the enemies, united to persecute him, who converged at his waking moment. This legion was formed for one purpose: to see that he died deep down under the earth's surface where God didn't see and didn't care.

But the devil won't get me! His thoughts churned in the narrow room with its light-green walls. "Devil . . . won't get . . . me," he murmured aloud.

A nurse shook her head as Stubby-Parvin Wakefield returned to his anesthetic-restless dreams. He was alone. The mine exploded. His buddies had sealed off the entry. Buried alive! Forgotten by God. THE DEVIL IS WALKING! . . . Stubby could hear him crawling over the face of the coal in the realm of darkness. Coming closer, closer. Stubby screamed for rescue. And no one came . . .

*

The weeks which followed the accident were the longest in Stubby's life, even though his buddies came to visit at his bedside.

"The company can't help but offer you a day man's job," Sam Polcheck, a former buddy, explained during a visiting period. "It's a cinch, with that stubbed foot, that you can't be a ton man no more. You're lucky at that. Ton men make more daily wages, but day men work at cleanin' up even on *idle* days. Company might even offer you a job on top."

This hope — the hope that he could escape, at last, Fear's Prison — helped speed Stubby's recovery.

Stubby's hope died young that day when, after his release by the hospital, he reported for work back at Dan Webster.

"Mr. Pharoah wants to see you in his office," he was told by an errand boy.

Stubby followed the boy across the shale-packed, smoke-streaked yard to the owner's frame office. There, beside the cigar-smoking Mr. Pharoah's desk, Stubby's hope was crucified.

"The mine can't be held liable for every accident, you know that," Mr. Pharoah explained. His bald head caught reflected light as he leaned forward to flick ashes into a metal dish at the edge of the green blotter on his desk. "Only because we want to maintain good relationship with our men do we offer you a job at all. We don't have to, you know. The risk you men take is all yours; we feel we're being generous to give you employment. So either you start breaking in as a mule driver, or we can't use you."

The old fear rose up to choke Stubby where he stood, favoring his stubbed foot in spite of all his efforts to ignore it. His disappointment at not being offered a job as a day man, or at least a jerryman, was hard to disguise. There was no choice.

"Minin's about all I know," he agreed to Mr. Pharoah's request while hating himself for having to appear docile, and hating even more the circumstances. In his mind he had the puffy Mr. Pharoah deep in a mine entry. He was fastening his strong, shovel-calloused fingers around Mr. Pharoah's white collar while trying to let him feel the choking-dread of the damp which could kill a man before he knew it was there. No, that wasn't right. Mr. Pharoah wasn't a man; he was a pink mule worn gray-black by long service in the sunless underground. Stubby was the driver with the longest blacksnake whip any driver ever had. And Mr. Pharoah, Stubby's number one mule, refused to budge. Stubby uncoiled the long whip and slowly raised his arm to strike. As reality — the knowledge that he was a maimed man, a man who needed a job — made him lower his arm; he held his hands in front of him like a small boy, twisting his cap.

"I'll report at Dan Webster in in the mornin'," Stubby said, his eyes half closed, not daring to look up to meet the gaze of triumph gleaming in Mr. Pharoah's eyes.

At first Stubby bore his degrading experience in silence. His old buddies tried to cheer him, but found the new Stubby had closed and barred a door of sullenness between them, his meaning as plain as the scar on his throat. The breach with Sarah and his children grew wider; hate rose up to fill the vacancy. And after Luke, his fourth boy, was born, Stubby endeavored to seek solace for his stubbed-foot misery in a moonshine bottle. Revenge, so strong and sweet that his lips smacked it like old wine, he found deep inside the mine. There in the black-vault passageways with shiny, jet walls, he was king on his mule-car throne. The ship was his scepter, and his legions he used to punish a world organized to persecute him. An almost monarch joy gleamed in Stubby's eyes each time he raised the whip to deal out justice, a justice that he felt was long overdue from God.

Stubby's sons who managed to live into their teens obeyed his orders to follow him into the mines. His surviving daughters married miners as soon as they were old enough to escape his dominance of wrath. The baby son, Luke, screamed lustily whenever Stubby went near him, which wasn't often. It was all Sarah could do to keep the children quiet during their frugal evening meal. When Stubby left for the town saloon at night, a mock form of peace settled. Sarah seized this opportunity to relax on the lumpy bed. Anxiety, fear of Stubby's black spells, lack of proper food, and the unending chain of childbearing had taken their toll. She grew weaker each month as another worry loomed up: what would happen to the remainder of her brood after she was gone?

Depression stalked the land that spring when Stubby was assigned to the task of breaking in a new mule. In more prosperous times the job would have fallen to a flunkie. Feeling lucky to have held a job at all with Green Valley, Jackson Hill, and Big Dirty idle, Stubby swallowed hard and began his loathsome and humiliating task.

A mule was trained to trip open the metal door which swung open and closed by means of overhead hinges. These passageway doors had to be kept closed in order that fresh air could be circulated to the miners from a central system. A mule learned to open these doors by butting the door with its head which was protected, for this reason, with a padded-leather helmet. After a few trips over a downhill practice run, set up for training purposes, and a few whippings for shying away as it approached the overhead door, a mule soon mastered the trick and never forgot it after that.

Stubby's new mule, after his days of such training, was taken on a regular run inside the mine. When the mule balked at the first door, he was flogged. He refused for the third time. When Stubby removed his miner's carbide lamp to lean forward to burn the mule's already welted, sore rump with it, the mule kicked back to send Stubby sprawling against a tunnel wall.

In his half-crazed condition, and swearing with every breath, Stubby took the mule away from the team, hooked the mule's tail-chain to a steel crossbar next to the roof, so that it could not get away, and uncoiled the dreaded whip once more from his own neck. The mule became Mr. Pharoah, Mr. Freeman, Mr. Bledsoe, and all the other company owners.

The mule, a symbol of all Stubby's hatreds, stood dumb and popeyed from the same fear which Stubby kept hidden deep inside himself. It pranced and shook its head from side to side, seeking in vain for escape. With every blow, aimed squarely to cut the animal in two, an oath escaped from Stubby's mouth to echo with the almost human groan with which the animal begged for mercy that did not exist. It tried to kick, but the roof would not permit the space to raise its rump from the mine bottom. After the blood began to drip in free-flowing ribbons, the animal stumbled to its knees and lay on its side, no longer protesting, no longer caring. Froth from the animal's mouth was not unlike that which dripped from Stubby's chin.

Stubby became exhausted. Then, with a pity he felt mutually — as both were dumb animals harnessed together by fear — then Stubby knelt to cup his hands tenderly beneath the dying mule's head. The animal, unable to understand why it had been chosen as a sacrifice on the altar of man's inability to cope with fear, flicked open its eyes in one last effort, never to close them again.

"Poor devil. Poor devil," Stubby cried as tears of self-pity rolled down his black face, honest tears that he did not realize he cried. "You had to learn. Just like me. But you wouldn't; you balked. I didn't mean to kill you, you poor b———. Don't you know that? Oh, my God, don't you know what it's like to drag a foot, to be scarred, to be so damned afraid that you go crazy with fear? That's what — CRAZY . . . CRAZY AFRAID that someday they'll find you down here in this damp, dark hell . . . and won't nobody care. Oh, God, you let them run the devils out of men and stuck them into some hogs that went and drowned. And what about us *coal-hogs?* What about us? What about me? . . ."

The death of a mule was a catastrophe in Dan Webster Mine. Mr. Pharoah explained that union or no union, Stubby could no longer work at Dan Webster.

After a period of time, Sarah gathered strength to make it to Sam Polchek's house to beg him to take up Stubby's cause with the union. The union met and voted to enact a stay-at-home strike to get Stubby a job in another mine. Jobs were tough to find, but mine owners knew that other mines would come out in sympathy with the strikers. Stubby was lucky to land a job as a mule driver at Pyramid Mine for a day or two each week.

Sarah managed to keep her brood together only by the charity of neighbors. Luke Nimrod was barely four, and Dinah was two, when a four-pound girl, a tiny beauty with a face so like what Sarah's had once been, was brought into the world.

"She wooks wike a wose," Dinah lisped in admiration of the tiny red bundle tucked into bed beside the exhausted, smiling Sarah.

" 'Et's call her that," the boy begged as he and his sister leaned over the foot of Sarah's bed.

"Okay, okay," Midwife Granny Freeman decided as another seizure of cramps made Sarah's face a dark map of crisscrossed lines of pain. "Call her Rose, maybe Rosie-Addie if you want, but clear out of here and let you' ma get some rest. Heaven knows it's little enough she gets from your pa, the no-good, drunken, mule-killin' . . . sorry," she sighed to Sarah. As Sarah raised a clenched fist to her mouth, to bite against the knuckles to keep from crying out a protest to the pain eating inside her, the children dutifully trotted out of doors.

"I know it's the code of the mine women not to speak ill of another's man," Granny said while folding a blanket scrap neatly before adding a lump of coal to the smoking cookstove on which boiled rags in an open foottub. "But that man of yours — that Stubby, well, if he don't get killed in a fight at the Last Chance or Barney's one of these nights, he'll be the death of you. A brood sow, let alone a woman, couldn't live litter-torn the way you are."

As little Rosie-Addie grew up, one star seemed destined to shed light into Sarah's sunless life. It came in the form of a present, a scarred piano.

"You know, Sarah," explained Miss Fowjers, a neighbor. "We're movin' our whole family to my son's, Ishmael, in South Bend. He ain't got room for the piano. It costs too much to move it, anyhow. So if you'd like, I'll have our menfolks cart it over here for your Rosie-Addie to learn herself on."

The piano became Sarah's fortress against Stubby's cruelty. When Rosie-Addie's tiny fingers plunked upon the keys, those pumpkin-faced keys with the ivory missing, to Sarah's ears an angel band was playing. The tears of pride tried to wash the hopelessness of life from Sarah's fading eyes.

And after two more stillbirths in the next ten years, Sarah lost the battle with pneumonia and found peace at last.

When Luke was old enough for Stubby to get him a job — "to start earnin' his keep in the mines" — Luke bolted, and ran away north one morning. To Rosie-Addie he gave his last penny; she promised Luke, as only a child can promise, to escape, too, when her time came.

Stubby, as Sarah was lowered into her grave, promised himself to straighten up.

For a while he tried. The burden of confessing that he was driven on by fear of dying inside a coal mine, and being shamed perhaps by other groundhogs, who laughed off their own fear, proved to be too much. He could never escape his lifer term in Fear's prison. As forced bravado became his coat of armor to help hide his defeat, time brought improvements to the mines. When cutting machines, safety measures, and motor-driven cars made mules obsolete for mine work, his fear grew so that he sought, and was assigned, a job more to his liking.

Love Stubby had been denied, so much that he found solace in denying it to others, tried to find a place in his heart. Motherless Rosie-Addie tried to warm him with her smiles, and tried ever so hard to master his favorite "ol' country" songs on her piano. When Stubby refused the girl's love, he turned it into yet another fear: that Rosie-Addie, too, would leave him like the others of his brood had done. She found the tinny, out-of-tune piano to be her only hiding place; in it she found a reason for living at all.

Into the music of the piano and the magic of the hymnbook that Mrs. Laban, a church-going miner's wife, loaned to her, Rosie-Addie poured all her fears, her joys, and the plans for a different kind of life. Her ability to play the piano gave her opportunities to escape Stubby and the home life they shared. There seemed to be no place to run to, nor was there another hiding place. She could talk to her pillow at night to say, "At least, here in Genesis County, I am near to my mother. She loved the county. As long as it holds what is left of her, I can never bear to leave it. Even if I am tempted to go wander in the wilderness . . ."

Perhaps her mother could hear her music as long as she remained in Genesis County; she could never leave, for here, where so
many of her loved ones rested in the company-owned graveyard,
was all of her family that were worthy to be loved.

World War II prospered the treasure chests of Genesis County
for a short while. Stubby's money, little of which Rosie-Addie
saw during her sixteenth year in 1949, went into the cash registers
of the saloon. By "settin' 'em up" Stubby tried to regain the lost
respect of his mine buddies. The rest of his money went for his
frequent visits to Garcia's alley to call on a widow of the town.
If Stubby noticed that Rosie-Addie tried to pick up his favorite
songs to play in order to please him, he gave no sign of it.

> *And he said, What hast thou done? the voice of thy brother's
> blood crieth unto me from the ground.*
> *And now art thou cursed from the earth, which hath opened
> her mouth to receive thy brother's blood from thy hand; When
> thou tillest the ground, it shall not henceforth yield unto thee
> her strength; a fugitive and a vagabond shalt thou be in the
> earth.*

Always the story of killing the mule followed Stubby in Genesis
County. The little animal had its revenge at last; a revenge that
would live longer after Stubby's body, or what was left of it, was
placed to rest in Genesis County soil, scarred throat, dragging,
stubbed foot and all.

I have heard people say, as they yet tell Stubby's story, that at
his funeral that winter the preacher made people think a little
better of him.

The preacher made quite a sermon out of Stubby's trouble
and how he ended up because of it. "When God sent Jesus on
Earth to die for our sins, God subjected Jesus to every weakness
a man can suffer except *fear*. Jesus was never afraid because He
knew He was God's Son. But Stubby never knew he was God's son,
and like those who refuse to accept this truth, Stubby was afraid.
So afraid that it made his mind sick. He figured that the scar on

his throat was the mark of Cain. We all know Stubby's fear. We know the way he died wasn't easy. Let those who mourn remember that God ain't goin' to be too hard when He judges Stubby, cause only God knows how he was afraid."

PART FIVE

Preacher Brother Gorby

The Genesis Tree in our garden figured in many
of the lives of our people. As the tree became the
symbol of Truth and its searchers, and only God
knows what is truth, it figured quite innocently
in the life of Rosie-Addie Wakefield, and in the
life of the man who loved her . . .

JOHN HEZEKIAH GORBY stretched his muscular arms above his head. The warm Tennessee sun filtered through the shutter to make a shadow-ladder on his young chest where hair, as black and curly as that on his head, grew in V-shaped thickness.

He hated the whiteness of his body. It marked him, he thought, as feminine here where farmers were sun-browned by field work. "And I am a man!" he flung at the cracked mirror of the dresser. He paused in fear that Aunt Tilde, in her bedroom at the other end of the second-story hall, would overhear and learn the secret he could never bring himself to share with anybody.

When, after listening a moment, the silence indicated he had not betrayed himself, he bent his trunk at the waist of his six-foot frame to see better in the mirror. He rubbed his fingers against the stubble on this square chin; the whiskers bristled warmth to the pink of his palm, filling him with masculine pride that tingled in his bloodstream. He half blushed as the warmth answered itself in his thighs; for in the many months since his brideless marriage to Widow Maude Powell, this was the only physical warmth he had known.

Had he not dreamed, in the long, sleepless nights of his Aunt Tilde-dominated youth, of his nuptial night? I will be gentle, he had promised himself, so gentle that my bride will offer me the petals of her lips. Her perfume will be exciting as the first purple iris that blooms in the row which stretches along the driveway from this frame house to the shale road out in front. She will be young, will arch against my heart and . . . *And what?* The mirror mocked him. *Nothing. Nothing at all.* Truth silenced him. His stomach strained to retch up this tormenting truth.

＊

John Hezekiah Gorby, now that he was in his twenties, could never quite recall his beginning. All that he accepted was what his then middle-aged Aunt Tilde had told him: that his impoverished parents died when he was quite young, and in the "charity of her heart" she had reared him.

"You'll be a fine, upstandin' preacher someday," she had promised him. He had learned at this early age that it was not wise to cross Aunt Tilde; her decisions were never questioned in all of his lonely boyhood endured in the world she created, a world of starched petticoats and a flat bosom under the black crepe dress on Sunday, and of the limp calico dresses on weekdays.

In this feminine-modest world, his earliest memory concerned the taste of the bitter yellow soap Aunt Tilde used to wash out his mouth when, at making spelling words, he had innocently copied an *r* into the word *beast*. To say "breast" must be as evil as defaming God, he remembered well. Not understanding, he knew only that it meant being sent up to his quilt-covered bed supperless in the musty upstairs room.

The following morning Aunt Tilde unlocked his door and stood, framed by the dark oak doorway, to half apologize. "You can come out now."

God would have to overlook her; she never knew she would have to raise a boy. Her dark hair was worn in a smooth sausage roll at her neck; her skinny arms were covered by the plain, long-sleeved dress she wore as the uniform of her religion. "I hope you'll never say evil again, John." Not once would she call him Johnny. "Ain't pleasin' in the sight of the Lord. I'd hate to see kin of mine condemned to everlastin' burnin' just for using lustful words. You be a good boy, and I'll set you up some hot-mush breakfast while you're a dressin'."

With the submission of the resigned child, John donned his blue shirt and overalls; he sat on the edge of his bed and reached under it to find his heavy shoes. Dressed, he clumped down the hall to the steps. He strained the muscles in the calf of his legs in a conscious effort to be quiet; but each board echoed in the large, weather-beaten, silent house.

"You'd wake the dead, I'll swan," Aunt Tilde greeted his arrival in her kitchen. She helped him wash his hands at the sink by pumping water over them from the pitcher pump. He took his place, opposite hers, at the round, oilcloth-covered kitchen table. "Be sure and say grace," she cautioned as he picked up a spoon when she placed the steaming ironstone bowl before him.

"Soon as you're through, I've got a erran' for you. Want you to go over to the Widow Powell's and borry some knittin' needles. I've misplaced mine, and I've this throw to finish for the preacher's wife afore the next Sunday the preacher's here. Wish we could afford a regular Sunday minister here," she stopped to aim the fly swatter, always beside her chair, at a *nasty pest* on the window, "but sharin' one circuit preacher, every third Sunday, is better than none — like it used to be. I can hardly wait for you to grow up, John. So's you can learn to preach!"

As soon as the boy was out of sight of Aunt Tilde's drab house, he shed the heavy shoes. Wouldn't she have a fit if she knew! The clover in the valley at the bottom of the hill felt like the balm of Cloverine Salve to his feet. The singing of his freedom was in tune to the humming in his chest. The stubble of the newly cut field, as he began the second mile, caused him to wince. Squatting on a hollow log at the edge of the woods, he replaced his shoes. The creek, where the bank was velveted with moss, gurgled invitingly, yet he plunged on. In the valley below the next hill he climbed, the Widow Powell's envied house spread its turreted, gingerbreaded, white-framed splendor in the sun.

The two-story house, where the Widow Powell had lived alone since her husband's death, was truly the showplace of this entire hill county. The eighty acres sloped up behind the house and were caught neatly in a snood of barbed-wire fence. Holsteins grazed in the pastures while the share-rented acres were bushy with the promised grain yield. If all these were mine, instead of just the patch

Aunt Tilde and me farms, John wished as he descended the hill, then me and her would be livin' high on the hog. Aunt Tilde wouldn't have to knit and piece for other people to keep clothes on our backs. But the Widow Powell's land's not our'n, and no way of gettin' it. His fists socked the invisible enemy — the accident of birth — deep into the pockets of his patched jeans, and the weight of jealousy made his eyelids feel lead-lined in the sun.

He thought about Maude Powell, the owner of these riches, and about the way people said she acted "queer." Many men had swarmed in from the hills to court Widow Maude Powell, knowing she would not be cold in bed, and that her money, if Henry left her any, was enough in itself to attract them. Old men; young men; farm workers in straw hats; dreamers in caps; scoundrels and schemers all alike, they came. They would smile at her and overlook her yellow, gold-crowned teeth, her too-plump-in-the-wrong-places figure, and her center-parted straight brown hair which had its monthly rinse in camomile tea to keep it dark. They had all come to sit — at least once — in the straight cane, chair on the purple-clematis-shaded porch in the summer. They had tried to make pleasant talk as she swung back and forth, alone, in the porch swing. "You need a man to fix that squeak," they would say.

"I like to hear it squeak. It's a purty sound for a lonely woman," she would reply, and flutter girlishly the fan which a long-dead niece had mailed to her as a souvenir from Niagara Falls. As her eyes glazed with that spirit-world distance, and as she knitted her crossed ankles together until the squeeze of her thighs beneath the short, tight skirt was obvious to her would-be suitor, she would talk. "My husband, the late Henry, liked anything with rhythm. Ain't never gonna change things round here from jest the way Henry liked 'em. Sometimes I know he'll come back. Weren't no man as big as Henry in this 'hull hill country . . ."

Her courters seldom returned the second time. The boy's hands sweated as he hurried along.

As John closed the iron gate behind him and awkwardly began his walk to the house, Widow Powell welcomed him from inside the dark cavern of the building. Keeping her house so dark, he wondered, does she have eyes like a cat's?

"Come in, Johnny Hezekiah," she invited. "A mighty purty boy you're gettin' to be. Don't come often enough to suit me."

Squinting from the recent brilliant sunshine, John entered the funereal-dark hall with its matching time-stained woodwork. Before his eyes accustomed themselves to his surroundings, she swept his body to hers in a smothering embrace. The odor of her cheap violet talcum mixed with woman-smells, and of his own wet sweat beneath his dusty denim shirt rose up to strangle freedom-air in his nostrils. He thrust back his head from her over-stuffed bosom; then recoiled from the playful nip of her teeth on his throat above his shirt collar.

When he struggled, she released him to the safety of the leather sofa. The pattern of the red-and-brown parlor rug came into focus. He breathed normally once more.

"Knittin' needles? Sure," Maude Powell laughed, much too girlishly for her forty-three years. "You'll fetch 'em back afore Sunday?" She bent close to him to silhouette against the violent grapevine wallpaper. "I'd bake you some cherry cobbler if I know'd exactly when it'll be."

She left him to walk through the huge arch leading into the dining room. Her hips swayed like plump goose-feather pillows beneath the tight short skirt until the glass beads, dangling from the green, umbrella-like lamp shade hung from the middle of the room tinkled. Her eyes narrowed as she looked back at him over her shoulder.

"Let's play a game, Johnny. You try to catch me and hold on to me afore I get to the kitchen. If you do, I got a reward for you, huh?"

She waited while he struggled to stand. His forward wobble in the heavy shoes was awkward. With little effort he reached her before she rounded the oak dining-room table. His outstretched arm caught her leather belt. Like a Spanish dancer she stopped, pirouetted back toward him so that his arm encircled her waist. One of her arms held him to her; with the other hand she stroked his dark hair which curled at his forehead. "Caught me, didn't you, you purty thing?" she crooned as if to a small child. "But you'll grow up, Johnny," she promised. "You'll grow up and be almost as big a man as my Henry was. And you'd enjoy what he left me, too. Left me well fixed, Henry did. They all know about the stack of bills. They all want 'em, but I'm too smart for 'em. I know what I want."

John stared at the green shades in the dark dining room. He had heard people talk about the widow's money in secret speculation. No one knew if it existed or where she kept it hidden. Only Lawyer Bennington, over in Freelandville, knew if there was any money; and knew that the rent from her land was more than enough to provide for her needs.

"I'll fetch you some milk from the cream cellar and cookies from the pantry. While you're waitin', if you promise to be good, I'll let you admire my bird-egg collection. Got all kinds, all colors. They're in that big glass bowl there on the buffet. Don't you bother 'em now. No feelin' 'em. Just look, mind you!"

Accustomed to obeying his elders, John walked to the buffet, curved his fingers over the edge of its polished oak surface, and stared at the huge cut-glass bowl of empty birds' eggs. Each tiny, fragile dome bore the pin-prick mark through which it had been sucked empty. Why would a woman like Widow Powell collect these bird's eggs which belonged to the world of small boys, and treasure them, empty, in a place of honor? But there were many odd things about Widow Powell which John, and those in the county, did not understand.

All of the pieces of the puzzle would fit together someday . . .

So . . . That a Grown Man Would Know Why . . .

Circumstances changed very little in the virgin-field years which John plowed through to become a man. In his thirteenth year the portly evangelist, Preacher Brother Chatman Root, had come down to Tennessee, all the way down from Genesis County, Indiana, to conduct the tent meeting at Freelandville. At this revival John felt, for the first time, his calling to serve God; he had surged forward with the crowd of the other admitted-sinners to be saved while kneeling in the sawdust around the Mourner's Bench beneath the pulpit.

At the meeting's close, Root baptized all the confessors in the river. On that day the customary basket dinner was served on the riverbank after the ceremony. The saints, the saved women of the congregation, loaded their Model T's, and their Model A's, and their family buggies, to endeavor to outdo themselves in filling the wicker dinner baskets with their best delicacies. The meal was a gesture of appreciation attending the departure of dear Brother Root, "to thank him for cleanin' out a passel of sinners in the county."

In his only white shirt, as the last of the sinners to be buried with Christ in the watery grave, John was immersed. He could feel Preacher Brother Chatman Root's strong arm supporting him as he was bent backward. An ache in his chest ballooned. Instead of increasing the pain, it exhilarated him beyond all sense of feeling for a brief moment! He shuddered as if in a chill — an involuntary shaking which the minister felt, too; felt it so that he found himself placing his own arms on the boy's shoulders to search John's wet face.

"It's the hand of the Lord on you, John Hezekiah Gorby," Root declared. "He be a callin' you to serve Him. You'll be a big man when you're grown, Gorby." Then he whispered, "And God's always in need of men who think big."

"I aim to be a preacher just like you!" John's voice quaked. "We been needin' a regular minister in this valley for years," he confided.

"Don't stay here." He looked up at the people gathered on the riverbank, waiting to congratulate the dripping baptized as they waded to shore, and to offer them blankets to cover their wet-outlined figures. "It is written that a prophet is not without honor, save in his own country," he answered the question in John's troubled eyes.

"Is that why you travel around, then?" John asked before they turned toward the shore.

"Yes. That's why I had to leave Genesis County . . . to preach the glory of God everywhere."

"But wouldn't you rather have stayed there?" John slipped sideways as a rock on the river bottom bruised his bare foot.

Brother Root weighed his words as if to caution his enthusiasm not to show. "Stayed in Genesis County? Exactly. It's a leftover Eden — the land of milk and honey. They even call the swampland Eden there. But I had reasons for leaving that you wouldn't understand now because of your age. You will someday, if you can keep the women away until then."

"Do you think I should go to Genesis County someday — this land of milk and honey?"

They emerged from the water as they approached the dry land. Root turned and appraised the boy's wet body. "Someday, perhaps. For it is indeed the land of the milked and the honeys," he said very low.

At that moment Aunt Tilde swept forward with a spread blanket for the boy's cover. She hustled him behind some convenient bushes to dress himself in the dry clothes she had brought along. All the while John planned to seek Root out, to ask him what he had meant by calling Genesis County, Indiana, the "land of the milked and the honeys."

But the clustering crowd milling around the preacher prevented John from getting close enough to ask the question which still puzzled him. As surely as the sun began to coax the blood to flow and warm him in the dry clothing, the man-about-to-be, inside him, promised that someday, when he was ready, he would go to Genesis County to learn the answer for himself — to become one of the searchers of Genesis County. And there was . . .

MUCH TO BE LEARNED IN THE MEANTIME . . .

In his teens John managed to attend high school part-time. Two miles he walked, and rode the bus for ten more. His teachers felt sorry for this awkward boy who seemed intelligent, yet withdrew himself from his classmates who seemed dedicated to the pointless laughter of youth; they gave him his credits, knowing that he learned very little. How could he learn equations when he read only from the Bible concealed in front of his Algebra book? Teachers consoled their actions with the thought: He is smarter than others in building knowledge inside himself where *neither moth nor rust doth corrupt.* With this education as his crutch, he began his long climb to serve at the foot of the cross.

He tried to grub his substinence from Aunt Tilde's tired acres by day. Evenings he chopped rough poles to form a skeleton shelter; the roof was a covering of green limbs. On Sundays, and three nights a week, he conducted his first services to glorify God in this brush harbor.

Alone, Tilde listened to his beginning sermons. The neighbor's children, attracted by the hymn-singing noise, came next. Cousins came to be followed by their parents and seated themselves on the split-log benches. A questionable musician, a reformed but often backsliding drunk, came forth to plunk accompaniment for the lusty hymns on his banjo. Inevitably the meetings attracted the community's rowdies. The boys, slightly younger than John, stood at the rear of the harbor and ad-libbed insults which sent themselves, and the tittery teen-age girls in the audience, into gales of back-slapping laughter. John, with all the false dignity which he managed to muster behind his assumed title, "Preacher Brother Gorby," one that every minister earned in the hills, felt the heat of their laughter like the August sun on the back of his neck.

"Oh, ye of little faith," Aunt Tilde chided him when he let his blush show his discouragement. "You just pray, John," she advised as they walked home one night. "The Lord'll answer you. What you need to pick up the spirits is a piano."

When his shrug protested his lack of money for such a luxury, she sowed the seed of her scheme. "We won't need money, John. Only one hereabouts who could afford to give that much money is the Widow Maude Powell, and she's up in Indianapolis taking a cure or her ailin' nerves. But she'll be back one of these days. I'll just take over a jar of my raspberry preserves, and come right out and ask her, when she comes back. She always did favor you, John; always let you look at her egg collection when others couldn't never go near it — or even get invited inside that big, purty house of hers!"

"I hate to have you ask her, Aunt Tilde. I'm past twenty-one, a grown man. But somehow I'm still afraid around her."

"Nonsense," Aunt Tilde soothed. "It's just that Widow Powell likes men — young men who are as purty as you — and has woman-ways, affectionate ways of showin' it."

"I know," John said quietly, his head lowered so that his face flushed with heat of embarrassment. "The word to describe men, Aunt Tilde, is *handsome. Pretty* is for girls."

"Then you are purty," Aunt Tilde defended. "You even look like a girl. Often wished you'd been a purty girl instead of such a purty boy."

Her tinder-words ignited the bonfire burning in his chest. Just because he was female-dominated, why did no one seem willing to grant him a male's privileges, or regard him as a *man?* He hated the long, low whistles of the tobacco-chewing boys who gathered around the harbor at night, their meaning all too clear.

Widow Powell came home that winter. Aunt Tilde waited until John had been called away to substitute-preach for a minister on the other side of the county, wrapped her jar of jam in newspaper, and made her way over to call on Widow Powell. There was no reason, she argued, for Preacher Brother John Gorby to let his dislike for begging stand in the way of a piano. At any cost.

"Why Maude Powell!" Aunt Tilde greeted her flatteringly when her knock at the door was answered by its owner. "You look as if you'd found the fountain of youth in Indianapolis! Hows on earth did you get back lookin' so young?" Aunt Tilde stared, astonished by Maude's crisp permanent and dye job, her painted eyebrows, and the bright new clothes skinned over her figure now confined by an efficient girdle. "Just wait until John sees you! I do declare how you look young enough to marry now. Often wondered why you never did!"

"Never found anyone I liked as well as your John, Tilde." Maude indicated a chair for her near the couch in the living-room parlor. "My hired hand tells me that they call him Preacher Brother Gorby now, and that he's purtier than ever. Always knowed, back when he was a boy and came here borrowin' things, that he'd be a looker. As big as my Henry was."

Not wishing to state bluntly the purpose of her mission at first, Tilde paused in her stiff leather chair to study the carpet at her feet. "He's changed in these three years almost as much as you have, Maude. My, I can just set here for hours in your parlor and admire you. Who'd ever guess with you lookin' about thirty, that you're past fifty-five?"

"Don't say that!" Maude shouted, leaping up from her seat on the leather sofa. "I am young! I am! You and those silly doctors saying I'm aging." Her eyes narrowed so that Tilde felt certain she was going to have an epileptic fit. "I'll never be so old that the boys won't look twice, and wet their dry lips with their tongues and wonder what it would be like to —"

"Maude!" Tilde interrupted with gained courage. "Remember you're atalkin' to a lady."

Widow Powell snapped back to Southern politeness the way a corset stave slips back into its seam; yet her copper-colored laugh which followed was an ugly brass chuckle which further dulled the artificial situation. "Sorry, Tilde. Got carried away I guess."

She finger-pressed the pleats of her satin skirt. "Everyone, you know, talks that open way in Indianapolis." She preened imaginary peacock feathers as she studied Tilde, the country hen, from underneath her coyly lowered mascaraed eyelashes.

In the nick of time Tilde remembered the object of her visit; it wouldn't do to speak her mind now. "But you do look real young, Maude," Tilde offered, brightly. "And I know you, with your generous heart knowed all over the county, would be willing to help out somebody else real young."

As she explained about John's need of the piano, she emphasized her play on Maude's vanity. "And John often talks about your bird-egg collection. Still says it's the finest ever."

"It is." Maude flitted anxious glances toward the arch of the adjoining dining room. "Wrapped each egg in cotton and kept 'em with me in the hospital in a box by my bed. Told the doctor not to move 'em 'cause the eggs were part of me. You can't be separated from the things that are part of you, can you, Tilde?" Maude's eyes glazed with the same look which made people call her "queer" for so many years.

"Guess not," Tilde agreed uncomfortably.

"Them egg's part Henry and part me, just as I'm the fer-tile part of 'em . . .'"

Tilde chose to ignore the remark which she couldn't understand; she was wary of getting Maude riled up again by asking for an explanation.

"Then it's all right for me to tell John that you might be interested in helping him get a piano for his brush harbor?" Tilde fumbled with the sweater she had draped over the back of her chair; for some reason Maude's manner made her feel chilly. Without knowing exactly why, she promised herself to hurry out of Maude's sight. She might even run part of the way home.

"Sure. Send John over on Monday night when he gets back. I'll be ready for him," she added significantly. "I've always got plenty — Henry provided for me — for that boy John. You always knew that, Tilde . . .'"

Tilde refused to let herself think things out until she was at last safely out of sight of the Widow Powell's tall house. A strange pain pressed on her stomach, much like the time the window fell shut on her thumb; she had popped the thumb into her mouth to suck hard, and was almost afraid to take it out to see how deep the crushing went.

It was better not to let one's mind dwell on what was already past. Seems Paul said something about that in the Holy Scriptures, she recalled to ease her mind. And after all, wouldn't it be nice if Maude would do all right by John with Henry's money? That is, if it really existed. She sighed. It might be the way the Lord was choosing to get money needed for His work. Maude might do well by Johnny, and the community, of course, in building a church in addition to the needed piano. Yes, sir. Johnny could do himself proud by picking off Maude and her money. Was it fact or just neighborhood fancy that Henry had left her anything but the farm? No one knew exactly.

By the time Tilde had reached the shale-road turn-off, which would put her within five minutes of her house, she decided that perhaps it would be wiser not to mention the strange change in Widow Powell to John. It would be better if he didn't hear about her changing moods, her double meanings and hallucinations about her . . .

Youth Being Everlasting

"I don't want to go calling on the Widow Powell," John objected when Aunt Tilde told him of the arrangements.

The round kitchen table, with the same oilcloth cover of his growing-up years, was between them. "She either wants to help, or she doesn't. It's either making a gift to our blessed Lord's work, or it isn't." The light of longing was so bright in his eyes that Tilde knew to press her plea with added fervency.

"You *do* want the piano, John? Well, did you hear of our Saviour complainin' when He carried the cross? God helps them that helps theirselves." She paused long enough for him to weigh facts.

"If there's enough of that money of Henry's —"

"Do you think that money really exists?" John interrupted.

"Just mightn." Tilde watched him as the wind watches the young willow tree; watched John's yearning build a house of straw. "She just mightn be charitable enough to build a church, too."

She turned from her forced lack of interest — gazing out of the window — to watch his eager face across from her. Feeling

the guilt of a schemer, she rose quickly to turn down the kerosene stove's smoking burner.

Slowly John returned his cup to his saucer. "A church?" he
asked in a hushed, prayer-like voice.

He clenched his fists and raised them to press against his chest.
Leaning forward, he rested his elbows on the table.

"Do you really think she would? A church for the hill here?
I would give anything. Anything, Oh Lord . . ."

The sun burst momentarily from behind the clouds to cast a
patch of light on the worn, linoleum-covered floor.

After a moment Aunt Tilde asked, while searching his up-
turned face, "Are you sure, John? Anything?"

He remained silent as he turned to sit backwards on his chair
and cradled his arms on the back of it.

Aunt Tilde looked out of the window in the direction of Widow
Powell's house. "If you're sure about wantin' a church more
than anything, you'd best be actin' like it. Go powder and perfume yourself up real good. If you're gonna ask miracles of the
Lord, it's only fit you should carry your end of the cross by helpin'
matters out a little."

Preacher Brother Gorby would never forget the hour of dusk
that night if he lived to be a hundred. It was revolting. The
smell of furniture polish, sour cream, must and decay of the years
was so blended and strong, it churned up with the bitterness of
nausea in his flat stomach.

Maude Powell was waiting, talons bared, for him inside her
dark parlor. She was watching the gold watch with the black
grosgrain strap on her wrist when he knocked at her door.
She came across the floor in a dress, saved from the early thirties,
of flesh-colored chiffon which showed her plump knees in front,
and cascaded in back in longer tiers. Generosity was spelled many
ways: the smile, the new perfume, the welcome.

Had she used the perfume to bathe in? he thought as the sicken-
ing scent bikinied up to his thin nostrils. For a choking moment

the urge to run and run and run, to let the door slam definitely behind him, was almost as strong as the scent. Fighting disgust, he made his toes take a firm grip on the soles of his shoes to restrain himself. There is no personal sacrifice, he argued without quarter, too great to further the work of His kingdom!

He took the seat Maude indicated, with great flourish of the chiffon scarf attached to the shoulder of her dress, beside her on the leather couch. As twilight felt into the room with its gray-fingered glove, Maude lighted a small table lamp which only added to the funereal look the bowl of dusty artificial roses on the table gave to the room.

John held his breath in the awkward, strange stillness. How should he broach the subject — the piano so dear to his heart?

Maude was as coy as a water moccasin in a minnow-rich creek. Bluntly she turned toward him. Her manner was the crude imitation of a bashful, but naughty country maiden.

"I suppose your church wouldn't like it if I offered you some of my famous blackberry wine? No? If you don't mind, I'll have some though. My doctors up in Indianapolis said it was good for my nerves."

She stood up and walked across the room, swinging her hips in an exaggerated fashion. "A woman approaching the full bloom of life has to put her health first," she said looking back significantly over her shoulder.

Preacher Brother Gorby ran a nervous finger under his collar. The room, as he watched her return to the couch, her concentrated effort to strain the curves of her body against the confining dress, became uncomfortably warm. She maneuvered to sit as close to him as clothing permitted as she sipped the wine from a water glass. Like a siren of silent movies, Maude placed one moist hand behind his head. With the other she pressed her glass against his lips.

"No one will know," she began, with the words that have been a woman's stock-in-trade since Eve first used them. Then, with the strategy as old as Achilles, she struck at the heel she knew would hurt him most. "And you'll be provin' that at last you're a man. You *want* to be a man, a man like my Henry was, don't you?" He found himself swallowing the sweet liquid that was a strange fire.

When she lowered the empty glass, she forced his head, still held by her firm grip, down so that she could brush the wine from his lips with her own and make certain he felt the ballooning pleasure. For the first time in his life. Encouraged because her attack was weakening his male defenses, she thrust again. "You'll know what it's like to be a man like Henry. For all the things that Henry had can now be yours . . ."

He remembered that his arms circled round her, that she had pressed her body against his, a practiced art, and that she had murmured against his lips. "You want a piano, Johnny? Why ask so little?"

And later, while he was exhausted and still trembling, she continued her attack. "Marry me now. Marry me and help me remain young forever, Johnny, and the church you need can be yours. All that Henry had can be yours."

The guilt of the embrace cooled the moment as if the fruit-cellar door in Aunt Tilde's kitchen had suddenly swung open. He released Maude and struggled to his feet. "Sorry," he apologized while the truth froze his tongue like the zero day he touched it to the metal handle of the well pump. "G-go-got carried away, I-I — guess . . ."

"Carried away, hell!" Maude stretched out on the couch to give him the benefit of her disarranged clothing. "You . . . a minister, lusting after the fleshpots! You'll marry me now or you'll never preach another sermon again!" She shrilled her accusations in purpling anger.

"But I never actually . . ." he began lamely, knowing she would not hesitate to carry out her threat which would silence his ministry forever.

Maude cried with Eve-inherited wisdom. "I'll tell that you used the request for a piano only as an excuse to come in here to rape an unprotected woman. People will remember your comin' here for years, and how I let you see my egg collection, innocent-like, not knowin' it was me you was after all of these years."

Her tears were ruining her mascara, making black streaks down her cheeks.

"A-all-right," he agreed as his trembling stopped. "Quit crying for heaven's sake. We'll get engaged if you say so."

His misery built a wall between them. Once again he was so weak that he wished frantically, femininely, that Aunt Tilde would magically appear to interfere on his behalf. Would he never escape from that feeling?

Maude smiled, sat up straight and smoothed her dress. "You're bein' sensible now. And you'll earn that church, the piano and some decent clothes." With a heave beginning at her heavy ankles, she stood. Couldn't she realize that her squinting eyes, above her mascara-streaked face, gave her the look of a circus clown after the last act of a bad season?

"Glad now I saved them Chinese silk pajamas of my Henry's. He never wore 'em much anyhow. Glad I found a man big enough to take his place."

Tilde, at least, was glad to hear the news when her nephew came home that night. If he expected sympathy for his action, he was cheated. Perhaps Aunt Tilde, he wanted to think, was so relieved that her plans were at last beginning to materialize, and that a needed church would be built, that she overlooked his need.

"Work on the church can begin next month," she said as she rubbed her two great toes together in her stockinged feet. "What could be better? Married in your own church, just think, John! Oh, it'll make your legs chafe a bit to know she's thirty-odd years older, but sure as shootin', you feathered you nest. Couldn't have did much fancier, I'd say, gettin' a church and all. It's God aworkin' for you, that's what."

So while Preacher Brother Gorby counted the days, Maude Powell counted the nights. While he invented a series of excuses to stay away from her house, she plotted to attract him there.

Alone. The wagging tongues of the community, once having recovered from the shock of the approaching May-December marriage, duly noted and recorded the number of "courting nights." The noose, he knew as the trapped wolf knows, was descending; Preacher Brother Gorby would hang himself. Permanently and pitifully. There would be no regret for his action in the commnunity for his loss. Yet who could not feel he was forever to be cheated: never to know what it was like to be loved as a man — and by a woman?

He found solace in the daylight hours, in the merciless heat of the sun as he labored beside the carpenters, the masons, and the volunteers to help build the pine church. Often in the moonlight he would return alone to the skeleton framework which cast web-like — the web of service from which he could never escape, nor wanted to —shadows on the earth. There on his knees, the scent of tarpaper strong in his nostrils, he thanked God for this miracle — a church to serve in the hill country and the valley — that was materializing at last! The joy of promise was a wine that made him drunk so that he tried to forget the price.

But when he stretched out on his bed at night, he was guilty of the sin of weighing, mentally, that price against the physical cost of taking Maude as his wife. He longed for the sting of the yellow soap Aunt Tilde had used to wash evil words from his mouth during his boyhood. The yellow soap was of no use now; there could be no turning back. The sheet beneath his back was suddenly wet. He felt the coolness of the sheet with the hand he had knowingly put to the plow. This *had* to be the Lord's way to serve Him. Had to be.

"There will be almost a year yet, Lord," he whispered into the darkness, "until the church is finished. If it's not Your will . . . there's still time . . ." The half wish, half prayer brought him sleep after a while.

There was scripture written on the pages of his dream.

For we are labourers together with God; ye are God's husbandry, ye are God's building.

Instead of the usual bridegroom dreams, the thoughts of no beginning and no ending were of the tiny frame building and the slender white latticed tower which would someday hold the bell to summon, forever, his people to worship. And when he dreamt the part where these same bells rang out to announce his dreaded wedding, he would awaken, sharply, to wipe cold sweat of dread from his forehead.

Blackberry seasons were used to count the time until the church was completed. His first sermon had been a success. Each of the pews, made of native lumber and placed in neat rows, seemed a symbol of the ladder-rungs he had climbed to success. Perhaps the backs of these pews would be scarred by the initials of young lovers who would later be united in this church. All these lovers would be his: for they would be the sum of all the empty love he could never give to a woman. The possessive look in Maude's squinting eyes grew until it squeezed him like a vise. Soon now, soon now. Soon. Was that what the wind in the oak trees was taunting?

Aunt Tilde scraped up the money, by diligent means, to buy him a cheap black suit from a Nashville mail order house. He had to hunch his broad shoulders a little to keep from straining the arm seams. The pants were an inch too short. Yet the suit did flatter him, made him *look* like a *man,* he thought.

He tried it on for Aunt Tilde that first time and watched his reflection in the hall mirror.

"God forgive me for my vanity, John," she sighed, "but you are a purty man. It keeps my pride up to know that when I hear there's still busybodies who say you're only marrying Widow Powell 'cause she obligated you with the church and all. No matter what's said, it's more Christian-like generous to give than to receive. By that," she paused significantly, "I mean that Widow Powell is sure 'nuff gettin' her money's worth."

She swept from the room, her cotton skirts swishing, before he detected her betrayal of any female emotion. This was his first glimpse that she cared at all about his future, and the knowledge, to which he had always been blind before, made the room seem momentarily brighter.

Had Maude Powell heard the whisperers' taunt? "He's marryin' that silly old woman just to get the church. Her and that crazy bunch of birds' eggs they say she keeps on that buffet. Why she's more'n old enough to be his mother. Thinks he'll keep her young, hah!"

Yes, she had heard in a half-ignoring sort of way.

To appear younger, she dieted until the circles under her eyes became hollow, dark caverns with webbed entrances. The contrast seemed to pale the color of her eyes which glazed so often now in those times when "she was not herself." She shaved off her eyebrows and drew them back as black question marks with eyebrow pencil. The white-streaked hair, hennaed to make her appear more youthful, was ghastly in association.

Her illness should have earned her pity if she had admitted it. Sometimes, for no apparent reason, all her energy seemed to disappear; she would be too warm and, as suddenly, start shivering as with chill. Women are supposed to be weak, she told herself, but I will not be a whimperer just to get attention.

The periods when sleep failed her, so that she would slip out of the house before daylight to wander alone in the woods, became more frequent. Still dressed but exhausted, she would fall across her bed and sleep deeply until almost noon. When day sounds awakened her she was unable to remember why she was sleeping so late, her fire-and-brimstone temper would flare up. Dishes once cherished and long hoarded would be broken and burned.

During one such spell, she brushed one of her precious bird eggs from the cut-glass dish onto the floor. She crushed it in a fit of anger, then sobbed for hours while trying, with childlike impatience, to glue the tiny fragments back together again. Failing, she rolled the pieces up into one of her dead husband's handkerchiefs, cradled it like a doll in her arms, and rocked it for hours while crooning, over and over, in a whine-whimper:

> "Ain't gonna get my Henry's money . . .
> No one, no one.
> It's for him and me . . . not nobody else's.
> No one's business.
> No one's no ones . . ."

Before exhaustion closed her eyes, she chose to open the handkerchief, pick up the tiny fragments, a piece at a time, place them on her thick tongue, and suck them into her mouth. And swallowed them. Her mouth flooded with saliva at their imagined sweetness, so that a slender rope of saliva trickled on her chin.

The wedding was set for twelve o'clock on Saturday. Her headache was worse because she had not eaten a bite of food on Thursday, and none on Friday, so that she could get her wedding dress zipped. The throbbing, even here in the early morning of her wedding day, seemed to volume up like the black cloud before a rain as she heard the awaited knock on her door.

"Come in."

Maude stood back to one side of the dark hall to permit Ben Bennington, her lawyer from Freelandville, and his wife Belle, who would be a witness to her signature on the will, to enter.

"Nice weather," Belle offered in conversation as her eyes gathered, in quick, positive glances the dark, secret interior of the house that had been the object of so many rumors these days. She noted the heavy leather furniture, the hideous rug, and the brass lamps just as she had heard, and smelled the must of their preservation. She blinked her eyes to accustom them to the gloomy interior so that she might also see into the adjoining dining room where the egg collection was supposed to occupy the prominent glass bowl on the buffet. But before she could get a good look, Maude asked her, pointedly, to be seated on the couch.

Lawyer Bennington had already drawn up the preliminary form. With a nod of his bald head he handed the will to Maude.

"Where do I sign?" she asked as she unclipped a fountain pen from someplace below the opening of her tight dress's bosom. Could the Benningtons hear the throbbing in her head, too?

"But surely you wish to read it all," he protested. "The listings — ?" This was not like Maude Powell at all, he thought; she had always been a finicky one — too finicky — on such legal matters before. "Just glance over it to see —"

"One thing I want to add," she interrupted. "Everything is to go to my new husband come-this-noon. I want you to put in, 'special, 'my entire bird-egg collection' is to go to the Preacher Brother Gorby."

"But it's already . . ." he began lamely.

Maude's narrowing eyes and tightening lips shut him up. She keenly watched as the words were written in, then signed the document with painful, careful letters.

Belle Bennington added her signature as witness in silence. It was true what people were saying about Maude, then, she thought as she watched her sitting there twitching her hands open and closed in her lap. (It was not unusual for a bride to be nervous on her wedding day, but wasn't it queer that she seemed to count each finger and then start it all over again?) Better not to make conversation which might rile her. She was glad when her husband stood up immediately, after completing his business, and offered the excuse that they must hurry back to town to get the will recorded before the courthouse closed at noon. They were relieved when her door closed behind them.

Only one person knew that Maude got the letter delivered to her box a few minutes after the lawyer had left. That person was undoubtedly the mother of an unmarried daughter who had sighed over the good looks of Preacher Brother Gorby; or a member of his congregation who honestly felt his sacrifice to obtain a church was too much, and intended the letter as a valiant, but underhanded, effort to stop the marriage. Maude brought the letter, folded on top of the daily paper, into the house.

She opened it with trembling hands, and spread it out on the dining-room table under the light of the overhead lamp with the green-glass shade still swinging its multicolored beads. The perspiration sat in tiny pillows on the faint hair of her upper lip as she read:

> Dear Mrs. Powell:
>   We don't wish to hurt your feelings none, but we advise you not to marry that young Preacher Brother Gorby. Our valley needs a preacher and a church. It was highly nice of you to build the church, but the difference in your ages just wouldn't make neither one of you happy. He will need a young woman to help him with the Lord's work, and God will appreciate no end your generosity. Hope you will not be offended by what we think is our duty as friend of you both.
>
>   Respectully
>   (No signature)

Maude frantically wadded up the letter. She smelled it, then tasted the corner of the sheet of paper. Her glance around the room was swift to make certain the unseen watcher, who existed only in her troubled mind, was not swarming in to challenge her action. Slowly she chewed the sheet of paper into a tiny wet ball and tossed it to hide among the birds' eggs in the glass dish on the buffet.

She pressed her fingertips to each side of her temples as the throbbing seemed to increase. Nothing would stop her now. Nothing . . . with the wedding only hours away.

In spite of the pain she drove herself on about the house, fluttering from room to room with a dust rag clutched in her right hand. "I'll show them who is too old!" she shouted to herself every time she passed a mirror. Exhausted she leaned against the door frame of the swinging door leading from the dining room to the kitchen.

"They'll not get him. They didn't get Henry 'cause the devil got him first — him and his cold feet. And they won't get the money either!" She lunged out to the kitchen, letting the door swing wildly behind her; there she poured for herself another waterglassful of the dark wine. And another. And once again

. . . the wine must make a good dream of . . .

PREACHER BROTHER GORBY'S WEDDING DAY

The white frame church was crowded. Children and older men, uninvited but dragged along by wives who "wouldn't miss this weddin' for the world," stood outside trying to see what was going on inside.

All during the ceremony Preacher Brother Gorby did not seek his bride's face, a mask of much-too-bright, careful make-up. Only when he placed the ring upon her finger did he notice the false fingernails, painted to match her violent purple lipstick.

He caught his breath in dismay — a minister's wife resorting to such false adornments!

Maude, mistaking his sigh for an explosion of long-smothered passion, impulsively lunged toward him to leave a purple imprint of her lips upon his chin. He burned with chagrin, unable to move, while the minister from Clay County, hired for the occasion, pronounced them man and wife.

To Maude, the amused titter of the audience magnified into gales of laughter. "Well, he's *mine*, ain't he?" she asked loud enough for all to hear.

Preacher Brother Gorby hurried her down the aisle. His face was divided in color: red for shame and a greenish-white-tense around the nostrils. The full impact of his sacrifice shocked him. The stone of Moses seemed to weight his chest. Wedded. No slight tingling of his thigh muscles promised the relief he had hoped marriage would give him. When they reached the door, he welcomed the handshakes showered upon them by the well-wishers.

He sat beside Maude at the table in the churchyard spread with food. The passing of time was measured by the lone pieces of blackberry, apple and cherry pie and the chicken, necks and gizzards only, which were left on the stone platters. The last of the light bread and butter had disappeared. It was after two o'clock when he helped his bride into the borrowed car and drove away into the hot afternoon sunshine.

Maybe it was fate that snatched the unwilling bridegroom from this great fear: the fear of being alone with his bride. Maybe it was a drowning man's straw he grasped so eagerly; but when they started to turn from the church driveway onto the shale road, Toad Hutcheson, a small boy with freckles on his face and warts on his hands, ran up to Gorby's side of the car. The boy's arms signaled frantically for the car to stop.

"Sorry, Maude," he apologized awkwardly when she overheard Toad's request. "It's a preacher's duty to go to the side of the sick when he is needed. I'll take you home and go on over to see John Hutcheson, since he's had a stroke and is callin' for me. I'll be back as soon as I can get away."

"You'll hurry?" she asked when she got out of the car in front of her house. "Remember that I'll be counting the eggs and waitin' for you, Johnny."

She turned to walk up the path leading to her house, pausing only long enough to watch his car churn out of sight around the hill.

If only she wouldn't talk about those silly empty eggs, he thought as he headed the chugging car forward. That's one thing about her I'm going to have to stop. And that make-up . . . half the town thinks she's crazy, anyway. He remembered how, after the ceremony, Maude had overheard the teen-aged girls talking; their young voices had drifted over from their gathering place behind the church.

"And did you notice," one soprano voice related, "how her eyebrows melted in all that grease? Boy, she's slipping in more ways than just her age."

Maude gallantly pretended she had not heard, but he had seen her hand automatically open her compact so that she could see, and with one frantic finger remove the stain dabbed below her left eye.

✳

But Preacher Brother Gorby couldn't begin to guess Maude's true feelings. He mustn't! Maude protested to herself as she walked up the path. He mustn't think me old!

The thought brought the old throbbing back to her temples until she was certain that the pain had been visible to the crowd which had gathered, in gossipy clusters, around the churchyard. Now, at last, she was away from the prying eyes of the congregation. Johnny, her bought-and-paid-for husband, would soon be back. And soon, she promised herself while she climbed the porch steps of her home wearily.

She skinned up the skirt of her tight dress as she hurried to the living-room mirror, sighed in relief as she released the hook of her squeezing girdle. The mirror confirmed her suspicions that the bright sun had been merciless to her attempt at artful concealment. She kicked off the pinching shoes in contempt.

"I *do* look old! I *do!*" she shrieked into the mirror. She felt the tone of her voice ascending with fever until it seemed to cook her brain. She struggled to control her shaking by walking into the dining room. While leaning on the heavy table for support, her mind raced back to the morning mail's anonymous letter she had hidden, a tiny wet ball, among the eggs in the dish on the buffet.

In her stocking feet she swayed over to search in the glass bowl for the paper ball. Failing to find it, she used both hands to dig into the eggs. Fragile, the eggs overflowed the bowl onto the floor. Could the letter have fallen underneath the oak buffet? But she needed a light to search for it . . .

Minutes later, in the kitchen, she rolled a newspaper taper, dipped the end in a kerosene can before carrying both back into the dining room.

Her attempt to squat down on the floor was prevented by her tight girdle. She sat flat on the floor and searched with the light of the taper. Disappointed at finding only stray eggs under the buffet, she tossed the paper torch behind her in her anger. When she struggled to get back up on her feet, the kerosene can got knocked over. Half in hunger, half in anger-weakness, she fainted.

In less than half an hour she recovered to smell the smoke: the heavy dining-room table was burning slowly. Aroused by her sense of danger, she stood only with much effort, not being able to remember how it all happened.

By instinct she clasped the glass bowl with its egg collection close to her chest and struggled to avoid the flames while making her way toward the front door.

"Henry, oh Henry, come. I didn't lose a one of them," she sobbed as she gasped for air. When she fell, just fifteen feet from the door, she was still crying, from a blank mind, "Henry, oh Henry, come. It's a lovely fire . . ."

Smoke attracted the people of the valley. The crowd urged Preacher Brother Gorby not to enter the smoke-belching house. He broke away through the line of the men of the fire-fighting bucket brigade and found his way to where Maude had collapsed in a heap on the floor.

In spite of her burns, and his, he carried her to safety. A member of the congregation drove them both to the county hospital while the rest of the neighbors continued to control and extinguish the fire before it spread to other rooms.

He was treated at the hospital for his burns and dismissed; yet he never left the hospital, sleeping when and where he could, during the next eight days.

Maude refused to recognize him completely, but each time he entered her room, she would whisper: "The eggs. The eggs, all yours now." He would nod his head in agreement, not understanding at all.

"And I *am* young, Johnny. You just ask Henry." This she would repeat while, with constantly weaving fingers, she braided the corners of the hospital sheet together.

Only because the doctor insisted that they needed her room so desperately for other patients, Preacher Brother Gorby, as Maude's only living kin, gave his permission to have her admitted to the sanitarium for the insane.

The months in which he occupied Maude's house alone grew into a year. He was at last driven back to the old house he had shared with his Aunt Tilde in his need for human counsel. With no more money to pay Maude's expenses, he sought her lawyer, Bennington, to learn that yes, there once had been considerable cash. But Maude had withdrawn it several years ago; must have hidden it somewhere inside their house.

Diligent searching with Aunt Tilde's help failed to uncover any money. But they did find the shoebox in which the neighbors had placed Maude's collection of bird eggs after the fire.

"It's silly the way Maude tried to save those bird's eggs." She held one up between her fingers to the light. "This feels heavy!"

Crushing the egg, she learned the reason. In each emptied egg, rolled so tightly so that the egg shell could be glued together around it, was a bill of large denomination! Maude's money was found at last.

The money provided for Maude's care after Preacher Brother Gorby left the county. His stature as an evangelist continued to grow for the seven years which followed his brideless wedding; his earnings went to provide for Maude when her money was gone. The county admired him for his loyalty (popular opinion was that he was merely doing his duty, and that his was a Christian gesture for which God would surely bless him). Thus Maude succeeded, with her insanity and dependence on him, in using these heavy chains to drag him down; her condition was his special cross to bear. Uncomplainingly.

> . . . and, as we are His people, the sheep of His pasture,
> the servant of the Lord wandered into . . .

The Greener Pastures of Genesis County

In his seven years of travel Preacher Gorby had learned to live in the feminine world of religion; had been pushed and dragged and fawned upon by widows and all good sisters who convened around each new town's tent meeting; had been stuffed with choice and experimental "vittles" until he learned to accept such inconvenience without a whimper.

Then, as if God had noticed his strange longing, the mail brought an invitation for him to conduct a six-weeks revival in Indiana's Genesis County. Without knowing why, in his mind he associated the county with achieving the status of manhood. Hadn't Chatman Root whispered, on the day of his baptism, that Genesis County was, indeed, the "land of the milked and the honeys"? Curiosity made him accept their invitation readily.

Perhaps in Genesis County he could prove he *was* a man. What would escape from the feminine world feel like?

Following directions in the letter, he arrived in the sleepy town of Jakeyville with its rows of taverns outlined in quivering, unsure neon. Idle miners leaned against the bank and post office buildings to watch the natives come in from miles around the town to do their "trading" and to eye any stranger passing through with an antagonistic eye. The mines weren't as active here as they once had been, and time was heavy on some idle hands. He arrived to park his black Chevrolet beside Shorty's Barber Shop, across from the post office, to inquire further.

The office itself was a narrow cell faced by two barred windows.

"You be the Preacher Brother Gorby?" the postmaster asked while a woman clerk peered, over his round shoulder from out of the gloomy interior behind them.

"I am," Gorby answered politely. "One who's proud to be in His service."

The postmaster wore a green eyeshade. With the eraser of the pencil he held, he scratched an ear which protruded above the eyeshade.

"Then I 'spect you'd better go see Bella Tennis, up at Howe's Corner. All the drummers stay there. Bella'll be boardin' you while you're here."

Following directions, and praying silently for the right words and gestures to make him acceptable to God and to these people he had come to serve, he drove up a shale road to a mailbox supported by a chain with links welded to make it stand rigid.

"BELLA TENNIS" the words on the box proclaimed. "LODGERS"

He parked his car in the neat driveway, got out, took his bag from the trunk, and mounted the steps to knock on the glass-topped door.

Bella, a puffy-faced once blond woman who wore rimless glasses which pinched her thin nose, admitted him only after peeking around the ecru lace curtain, of course.

"Breakfast comes with your room," Bella explained as he followed her up the steps of the two-story white frame house on the hill. The room she showed him boasted two windows facing out over the barnyard, but he could see that a good view of Jakeyville and its narrow streets stretched behind it. "The town's women-folks are already vying with each other for the honor of feeding you your other meals," Bella confided. "Won't they dust the cob-webs fast when they see we-un's got such a looker for our meetin's!"

At least Jakeyville's people were honest, if not tactful, he learned.

When the meeting got under way, Preacher Brother Gorby preached with the fire of religious anger in his eyes, the conviction of being in his heart, and the love of God for all living things on his tongue.

Coon Dog Creek, where the tent was pitched, had its congregation run true to form. As usual, the parents of marriageable daughters found reasons to consult him for special advice and prayers; these enlisted the aid of Bella Tennis, who made various attempts, during breakfast, to gain information on his marital status.

"With your wife in an asylum," Bella puzzled the situation while she absently added two more spoons of sugar to her coffee, "you're married legal-like. But if the tragedy happened right after the ceremony, then you're still — er — well, you're still a bachelor, you might say. Too bad you can't divorce her and still be a Christian."

"But the Bible is plain about adultery. God's word, you know."

Bella shook her head. "Sometimes the ways of the Lord are sure puzzlin' to us poor sinners."

"Indeed they are, Mrs. Tennis," he agreed as he poured milk over his oatmeal. "God is all-wise in His way of teaching His witnesses. Someday we hope to understand why these trials exist."

"Maybe it's a good thing we don't know why they exist." She gestured by holding her fork, prong upward. "Now you take that little Rosie-Addie Wakefield who plays the piano at meetin'. Ain't but sixteen, but her ma died in childbirth, and her pa, Stubby, ain't got all his marbles either, folks think. Stubby beat a mule to death back in '29, in a deep mine, and he's never been right since. It's a pity how he spends all his money in them hell-hole saloons. Flickers all he's got comin' from one pay to the next. There's no one to look after Rosie-Addie — 'cept her neighbors and the church — and her such a purty thing, too. With that dark, curly hair afallin' down round her shoulders, and her skin so white, she looks like an angel up there when she plays the piano."

"She's a charming child indeed," he sighed as he buttered his toast and hoped he was successfully hiding his own emotion. "It's a shame something can't be done. Welfare or an institution."

"That's it, Preacher. You know how the miners are. They're a purty close-lipped bunch . . . stick together, you know. What was it that writin' fellow from Terre Haute said, that Debs, about them livin' by a code of their own? Don't remember 'xactly, but Jock Wilson said the same thing, only different. Well, it doesn't matter none now, anyway, 'cause they don't live round here no more, and that makes a heap of difference in what you say about people.

"And Rosie-Addie's pa is no different. He rules her with an iron hand. She's afeerd of him, too. But not one neighbor would interfere with what goes on in their shanty. Only thing ever skeers

Stubby is that when she gets old enough, she'll run away and leave him with his own work to do. He'll never let her marry even if she wanted to. A shame, too, she'd make a good wife for a God-fearin' man." Bella reached across the table for a toothpick.

A good wife? Hadn't he thought of that as he watched her take a cue from his uplifted arm to begin the singing each night? Hadn't he unconsciously held a pillow to his chest just last night as he stretched out on his bed; and, when he found he was pretending it was Rosie-Addie, had flung the pillow from him? Hadn't he tossed until dawn's faint-heart hours asking God's forgiveness for his lusting after flesh? . . .

Rules were made to be broken, even in Genesis County, he discovered. That night, after the meeting was over, he asked to walk Rosie-Addie home. It is because I have sympathy for her and the squalid way she must live, he told himself, and because God has blessed our night's meeting by bringing nine more sinners to confess their guilt at the Mourner's Bench.

Her worshiping eyes opened wider when he gained courage to ask her. Lowering her tassel-fringed lashes, she consented. "I just hope Stubby, he's my pa, ain't home yet," she murmured.

They walked for a while with the wall of nothing-to-say separating them. When he took her arm to help her at a curb, felt her tremble and grow stiff at the same time, he knew that her trembling was from fear — a fear that would grow and multiply within her until this Rosie-Addie would become like the gob separated from the salable coal and cast aside. He didn't kiss her that night, nor did he the next, though he found himself wanting to. Desperately.

The letter from Aunt Tilde made his hope mount. The hospital had notified her of Maude Powell's serious condition, and that her hours on earth were numbered, owing to hemorrhage beyond control.

He held the letter in his hands for a while. When he searched himself for a feeling of honest emotion, he found it was in vain. Instead he was filled with a great wealth of peace that comes to those who have faithfully kept vows, and have borne their cross in humility and silence.

That night he kissed Rosie-Addie for the first time.

A week later Rosie-Addie went with him to fulfill an after-service request for bedside prayer at Sister Gerke's block house, a shack like the others which the Green Valley Coal Company had built for its workers on the flatlands.

After the charitable mission was accomplished, they left. Rosie-Addie preceded him on the path leading down the hill. The white moon swam behind a cloud and surfaced again on the other side. He reached forward to hold aside a bush branch so that she could pass without being scratched, and felt the brush of her cotton skirt against his legs.

"Have you ever thought, Rosie-Addie, of leaving Jakeyville?"

"Oh, no," she replied without hesitation. "In spite of Stubby — how we live — I'll never leave here where I was born. There's just something about this place that holds all of us here." She paused for a moment's contemplation. "I guess I couldn't live if I left Genesis County. Ever."

"Not if you loved something . . . someone . . . more than the county?"

He stopped to take her warm hand in his, there where the path curved gently around the barn. They could smell the cut hay, piled, waiting for the balers. In the night's silence they could pretend to hear the moonlight drenching the barn and the cornfields with the gentleness of rain.

Rosie-Addie pulled away. At sixteen she knew, as any woman knows, the question he would ask. She stepped on a loose rock in the path and felt her ankle twist. The next step made her wince. She dropped to sit on a pile of hay to rub the pain and to examine the ankle where a slight swelling was evident.

"Could I help?" He bent over her, half afraid to touch her; yet more afraid not to; for wasn't it the duty of a man to look after the weaker woman? His arms convulsed in indecision, then returned to dangle, limp, at his sides in his confusion. He couldn't trust himself this close to Rosie-Addie . . .

I am almost twice her age, he argued with his torment. I preach against the sins of lust. Even if I can, at last, be free to marry her, she has already told me she could not, would not, leave the county. "I guess I couldn't live if I left Genesis County," she said. And all the while knowing that a strange rhythm had begun to drum inside her. She had confessed that she feared and hated Stubby — breaking a commandment given by God; but still she could never leave the strange and mysterious tentacle-arms of Genesis County. Why must I lack the attraction this soil holds for her?"

The knowledge that he was legally still Maude's husband, and that he lusted after Rosie-Addie, stung him. Knowing all this, he lacked strength to run from temptation. Confession of guilt is still good for the soul, he argued in further confusion as he fell forward to his knees in the hay beside her.

The moon settled the argument by discreetly retiring behind a cloud.

" . . . let no man put asunder," he breathed upon her throat the promise. And that was enough; for he knew, now, that he *was* a man. A capable man.

Discovery often takes a heavenly path. Sometimes it tips a balance ever-so-slightly in favor of deep despair, so that we walk in fear of consequence — an inborn fear that sin will find us out. Could this be why we often view . . .

DISCOVERY WITH FEAR?

Rosie-Addie's father, Stubby Wakefield, who leaned on the linoleum-covered bar of Jakeyville's Last Chance Saloon, took out his bandanna, wiped the sweat from his forehead, and plunged the handkerchief into the rear pocket of his overalls. Stubby looked older than his fifty-four years; it was due, Stubby bragged, to his drinking habits of almost forty years, "As many a year as I've waded in an entry, I've waded al-ky-hol."

"You've had enough, eh Stubby?" The bartender was stern as

he watched from his side of the bar. He remembered all the times when Stubby had wrecked the chairs and tables before his mine buddies had had to carry him home, out cold, to sleep it off. (Rosie-Addie had learned to stay out of the house until he was sober; the many beatings with his cane had taught her that.)

"I'll say that. Say when I've had enough!" Stubby protested. "Ain't no b—— in Genesis County big enough to tell Stubby Wakefield that."

"But your credit's no good," the bartender reminded in an experienced, patient tone. "You're broke."

"Hell I am." Stubby sighed while rubbing the week-old stubble on his tobacco-stained chin. "If I'm flickered out, I'll borrow from my buddies. Hey Polchek, you s.o.b.," he hailed the squat, dark-eyed miner who stood at the far end of the bar where the green neon light reflected in his patent leather hair. "Need a buck."

"Just got two bits," Polchek answered. He moved toward a half-filled booth; with the rest of those who worked Stubby's shift with him in Number Seven, he knew enough to stay clear of Stubby when he drank too much.

"Then let's have it." He laid his cane — the one he carried constantly since that slate fall, the accident of years ago that had earned him the name of "Stubby" — across the bar.

Other miners in the narrow damp-smelling, hall-shaped cell of a room turned to watch the argument they knew would not end, at least not without excitement. Sometimes the miners had to fight each other out of plain boredom; so one with reasons drew their attention like the shrill signal that a cage was coming up to the surface.

"Why don't you just flip the two bits on bettin' Stubby, eh Polchek?" The dapper Slim Dominic fingered the new sideburns he was growing to match the tiny Hitler mustache and slowly arose from one of the booths in a row opposite the bar. "Why don't you bet Stubby'll be a grandfather 'fore he knows it?" Slim egged the battle on.

Stubby sobered as much as his fogged brain would permit.

"What the hell you sayin', Dominic?" He grasped the cane instantly to swing it over his shoulder. His back was flat against the bar.

"Wasn't anything, Stubby." The bartender tried to smooth things over; he tossed the bar-damp towel over his shoulder to indicate that he was there to prevent repetition of other times when such fights wrecked the interior.

But as surely as the dreaded killer, the White Damp, would creep along the tunnels in the pits to choke its victims, Dominic, who coveted the calm beauty of Rosie-Addie and would like to have had her for himself, wouldn't be quieted now. The dynamite shot had been wrapped and stamped in the hole, waiting to be fired.

"When I seen Rosie-Addie with that preacher saying good night on your shanty porch last night, he sure looked like he was gettin' his," Dominic taunted while nudging the men who stood behind him.

Polchek joined the miners grouped together to push farther away like sheep glued together when danger threatens.

Dominic, like a trapped animal, afraid, but not daring to show it, laid his head back to roar coarse laughter — the same laughter in which all human beings indulge when they are afraid to cry. Dominic laughed alone; his laughter almost echoed in the silence.

Stubby became as another animal with the same predatory instinct of every miner in the county to protect the young. No one could muddy Rosie-Addie's name. Not that her name was important to Stubby, but if he didn't make Dominic take it back, thus proving it a lie, Rosie-Addie would hear it, and might use this as an excuse to leave him. Then who would there be to do up the work in his shanty?

The fat was in the fire. The word "fight!" spread action into the other saloons like a miner's whistle-warning. But as the crowd began to gather both in back and in front of the Last Chance, a small boy pulled away from the edge of the crowd. He walked rapidly at first. Once safely out of sight, he ran.

The legs of nine-year-old Paul Porter were strong enough to carry him rapidly to the clearing where the tent was pitched.

Luckily those who had knelt that night for special healing prayer were leaving, so Paul hesitated at the rear flaps of the tent as they were being lowered for the night.

Preacher Brother Gorby smiled and extended his strong hand. "Missed you tonight, Paul. After you follow Jesus in baptism, you should give Him your presence, too."

"And didn't you say we were all brothers now in Christ, and that I am to be my b-brother's keeper?" He puffed because he had run.

"That's right. But catch your breath a minute, boy."

"Had to hurry . . . Preacher. I want to be jus' like you when I get growed. But if you live to see it, you and Rosie-Addie better run like hell 'fore her pa, Stubby, finds you! Dominic and him's fightin' in the saloon. Slim was blowin' off about you'uns. You know how miners fight to protect their womenfolks? Well, I figure Stubby'll be after killin' you if he lives over Dominic's beatin'."

So that's how it happened, only two weeks after he had dared to love Rosie-Addie, that Paul Porter warned them. Hours later Stubby staggered, bleeding and bruised, home to his shanty.

Stubby never knew that the shanty was empty, for there, where he fell on the porch, he was as dead until noon the next day. The flies swarmed over his mouth and the ants made pilgrimages up his pants legs; yet the neighbors dared not offer him comfort. They kept a safe distance and prayed silently, during the fitful moments when he half awakened to mumble-roar, "I'll kill that b——Gorby when I find him," that Rosie-Addie and the Preacher had put enough miles between themselves and Genesis County so that Stubby would never find them again.

For one killing called for another in the land where the miners slept during the darkness and worked in it during the day. Here the light would surely be slow in coming: that is if it ever comes at all. Until then the code of silent self-protection will not change. Until then they will cut each act as a dark cloak from the same old pattern, throw the cloak around the black shoulders of the deep earth in the hope of hiding away from those . . .

Who Can Forget the Killings of . . .

Rosie-Addie and Preacher Brother Gorby fled from Genesis County and were married in Kentucky, two days later. The fear of Stubby was replaced by the fear of God and His knowledge of their sin. Yet after a while, knowing that God can, and does, forgive the sins of the flesh filled them with a great fullness. A peaceful, unexplained fullness that asked this and nothing more.

The love of Rosie-Addie made him whole. If his sermons had been strong before, now, with Rosie-Addie beside him, intense in her beauty and devoted in her love for him, they became as invincible as a metal that no heat of man-made furnace could distort. The Lord walked with him and blessed his knowledge and manner of delivery.

Sometimes he would wake up during the night and spread his hand along the blankets to make sure that he still lived on the earth and was not awaiting his turn to view the Heavenly Father on His throne.

"How long, how long? oh, Lord," he would ask in the darkness because he could not believe his blessing. As a man so driven, he successfully led hundreds of converts to know his God.

Only one shadow fell across the earth-heaven: Rosie-Addie longed to return to her beloved Genesis County, grieved for it day after day.

She would begin the sunny day by saying: "It's a lovely day, isn't it? I remember one such day back in Genesis County where the lilacs bloom along the fence at Lake Shakamak," or "About this time of the evening I used to sit on the shanty porch and watch the kids gather lightn'n' bugs to fill the Mason jars they carried. There were all the families represented. The Asburys, the Bollingers, the Roots, the Hawroths and the Millers." Her voice would rise in her longing, and fall low to a whisper when she found him turning his head on the pillow, guessing that she was so homesick for the county.

"Oh how I wish I could take you back, Rosie-Addie." His voice warned without meaning to betray. "Your pa . . . we couldn't."

"It's not Pa I miss," she explained as she turned on her side and drew his head to pillow it upon the curve of her arm. "I know Stubby would kill me if he found me, so I can never go back. But I do miss the county. I miss the Sunday afternoon 'sings' they hold near Coon Dog Creek, and the neighbors all agreetin' me when they're aborrowin' and lendin', like nowhere else in the world quite like Genesis County."

"I wish there was a way we could bring part of it with us. For you to keep always."

She waited a while, groping for a way to broach the idea which had long simmered with her lonely, yearning longing. "There . . . there might be a way I could have something of my county with me."

His silence discouraged her. Would he love her enough to take such a risk?

"You've accepted that invitation to hold a revival in Evansville comes early spring. It's within a day's journey of Genesis County with time to spare. It would make me mighty happy if . . . "

"If what, Rosie-Addie darling." She moved his lips up to kiss her throat. "If what could make you happier with our child coming in the spring?"

"Well," she recited as she had planned to recite so many times before, but had lacked courage when she remembered her father's anger and the miner's code of revenge. "I wouldn't be able to go with you, so I'll stay at Mrs. Schloot's Rooming House while you go up. Remember that I told you Bonnie Miller had that Genesis Tree she brought over from her cousin's grave? — the one told about in the legends? It's the last one left. Well, you just slip out to Bonnie's house, and whisper to her what you want it for; she'll give you a start of it, I know, for she'll be glad to do it. Be careful. Don't let anyone see you going or coming, so as they could tell Stubby our whereabouts. Then you could slip the start back to me. I could keep it alive in water until the revival let out, then take it with me back to your Aunt Tilde's to await the baby's coming. To have a Genesis Tree of my own, from my home county, would give me a lot of comfort . . . almost like being home, close to Ma."

Why did her body tense with sheer joy as she planned the project of obtaining a Genesis Tree for her very own? he puzzled.

He didn't hesitate for long. How little her request; how exactly like her to compromise unselfishly so that he might continue in the work of the Lord as he saw fit.

"If it would make you happy, Rosie-Addie," he promised.

How could he refuse? She had never asked for proof when he had told her he was free to marry her. He had never shown her Aunt Tilde's letter that had reached him too late: he had married, not knowing that Maude Powell had lingered for three days longer before she died. Rosie-Addie would never know he had added the sin, innocently, of bigamy to his others. He had married Rosie-Addie, had loved her intensely, but was his love going to be enough to take the place of her childhood home? Or was there some strange justice in the feeling that Stubby must, somehow, still hold for his child, which drew Preacher Brother Gorby, much against his better judgment, to return that early spring day to witness the siren call of Genesis County?

Gorby waited until the meeting near Evansville had well begun. He left early one day to steal away, secretly, back to our town of Jakeyville. He kept off the highways, confined his traveling to the back roads so that he could not be seen by people who might remember him.

I remember the day very well. I was stretched out on my bed in my room. When his car stopped beside the garden fence, I propped myself up on my elbows to watch him look around, hesitate, then climb our steps to knock on our door.

Like all the others, he followed Mother out into the garden. I couldn't hear what they were saying because the weather was so nippy that my windows were closed. But I saw Mother question him in an intense, sympathetic manner before she cut a branch of the Raintree she loved so much, wrapped it in newspaper, and handed it to him as if it were the answer to a precious question they were asking each other.

What could they have been talking about? I didn't have long to worry on that subject, for Cosey Walters, wearing her galoshes which were splashed with red clay — the signs she had been out gathering poke and dandelions for a mess of greens — chose that moment to come down the road on the opposite side.

Cosey strained to see the man who stood with his back to her. After a minute's pause, she walked ten more steps toward his car, bent to see the license plate, then hurried away, retracing her steps in the direction of Jakeyville.

Mother would never have betrayed his secret. She didn't tell me who he was, nor did I ask; for I would hear about it soon enough. Cosey, I knew from experience, would not stop until she hit Main Street with her news. Why did she have to tell it before anyone else? It was her bid to importance . . . for what else did she have in all of her lonely life, the life which placed her on a stage of her own making, to feed her vanity upon? . . .

Cosey's discovery spread like honey on hot bread, for the county as yet had had nothing quite as juicy as the elopement of Rosie-Addie and the preacher to talk about.

Stubby had the news brought to him as he was leaning on the bar at the Last Chance. His mine's pit had been down that day while they sealed off a dangerous entry. His glass had been lifted so many times this morning that he was well on his way toward feeling no pain. He borrowed a car to herd across a highway and to break speed limits. It was a simple matter to find the rooming house where Rosie-Addie, left behind because she was too heavy with child, in her seventh month, to travel.

Stubby pushed his way into the house where Rosie-Addie was staying; he didn't bother to knock, for he had seen the owner, Mrs. Schloot, leave the house with a shopping bag in her hand.

He came upon Rosie-Addie taking a nap on the dining-room day bed. Rage, when he saw her condition, and not knowing that Gorby had been freed by Maude's death to marry her, flamed up to a white heat which added insanity to his drunken anger. He raised his cane high in the air to strike!

When the blow awakened her, still half asleep she struggled to sit up. Stubby slapped her down. With the advantage of the surprise attack, she could not escape the vicious beating.

When her cries faded to a whimper, he staggered back down the steps as he left, missing some in his blindness. Exhilarated by the vengeful feeling that he had at last defended his honor as a father, he didn't look back.

Mrs. Schloot returned from her trip to the grocery to find Rosie-Addie unconscious from the beating.

When Rosie-Addie died, two weeks later, in the hospital along with her child, why did Preacher Brother Gorby return to bury her in her beloved Genesis County? Was it because he knew she could find peace here with those she loved. Or was it because he knew that we who are born here can never really be separated from it?

Her funeral was private. Stubby didn't come to join the procession which climbed the hill, but Cosey watched for him just in case. It was Cosey who reported how Gorby had cried "just like a baby" at Rosie-Addie's grave; how he had turned away immediately, and not looking to the right or left, had entered his car and driven "clean out of the county."

They say that Preacher Brother Gorby was a different person after that. He returned to his preaching with greater understanding; his heart was fervently grateful for that short time he had had with Rosie-Addie, and that he had known — at last — a product of the land of milk and honey, the land of Chatman Root.

When he thought of his loss, his great fists would clench until the nails would bite into his palms. He fought the hatred of Stubby and prayed about it, often deep into the night. The churches which called him grew larger and stronger because God became strong in him.

"And not because, oh Lord," he often prayed in his bed, "not because I dared to love a miner's daughter who loved Genesis County more than her life, and that of my child, but because Thou hast seen fit to make me a man at last . . . the kind of man who must not turn back once his hand has been put to the plow."

Some tell that later on he sought Stubby out as he was leaving the Last Chance one night, to tell him he forgave him for beating Rosie-Addie, and — according to what was told — for murdering his wife and child. They tell the story especially when a new revival starts in town, or while the men are waiting for a payday to roll around and are out of drinking money. They tell it when they carry another citizen to his final resting place up on the hill.

When they come to *that* place, they will nudge each other and bare their heads in gestures of respect, just halfway up the hill. One of the miners will voice what they are all thinking about, but would rather not mention it aloud, for it violates their code of silence about a miner's private affairs.

"About here's where they found Stubby — what was left of him — on that early zero morning we had that fall. He was frozen stiff after a wolf, or maybe a hungry wild dog had got at him. He had got to comin' up here alone 'bout every day or so . . . like he was tryin' to prove he loved Rosie-Addie, and was sorry he beat her so she died. Funny thing about them both restin' here. Now both of them's sleepin' in peace in Genesis County where they wanted to be, but they never could find any peace here when they were livin'. 'S funny, ain't it? Like maybe God uses death to draw people closer together."

"Sure is," another miner will vouch. "Maybe it's a good thing the Lord planned this dyin' business, after all." Then the pall-bearers will get a new hold on the casket and carry it up along the path that they themselves will soon be carried over.

Yes, Rosie-Addie's story of elopement with Preacher Brother Gorby is still told around the fire in the country stores when men gather, on winter nights, to fry spit on the sides of the pot-bellied stove. I have heard it retold on the town bench across from the post office, and often in our living room.

And, as one of the searchers of Genesis County, I can't help wondering if things wouldn't have turned out differently if Rosie-Addie hadn't wanted a piece of the Genesis Tree, had wanted it so much that her husband had risked discovery to venture up here to get it for her, just as Eve tempted Adam to take, also, of the forbidden fruit. No, I don't know what attracts them all back to Genesis County. And maybe it's not knowing that will make me continue the search.

PART SIX

Myra

In my notebook the words multiplied as the Courthouse clock multiplied minutes. Here pages marked sums, subtracted reasons, and divided Genesis County into haves and have-nots. Why did the riddle's answer seem just beyond my grasp? The Bible says that the beginning of wisdom is the fear of the Lord. Was wisdom the answer of

> ... hope of a tree ... Though the root thereof wax old in the earth . . . Yet through the scent of water it will bud . . .

> . . . But his flesh upon him shall have pain, and his soul within him shall mourn.

And here, in the Genesis County I loved, this beginning of wisdom came to . . .

MYRA

I HAD REACHED the point where I could now judge the people around me by their stories, but happiness was not mine. The riddle persisted while my searching was as restless as ever.

In my early teens I began to question the wealth of this "Promised Land" in which I had lived. Time made the dim, flower-filled woods fade; brighter grew the scenes of Jakeyville's accepted poverty. Facts at last belched forth like sulphur gas from the deep ebony mine pits and brought the past with them. I listened as old miners told the coal stories, told how the black diamonds were torn from the Earth's giant ribs and hauled to the surface, told how the naked, coal-dusted, laboring miners were chained to the dark caves, and how the owners weighed each diamond-lump on a giant scale, paid for the miner's sweat, and smiled at the rich profit. Truth's accusing finger drew a line in the coal dust to divide this into the land of the haves and the have-nots. Beautiful Genesis County was torn and ugly before my time; I had been too young to offer protest.

The Genesis Tree, ripped, stripped, and shredded, died. Its heart, its almost human heart, had bled too often. Too many, asking too much, had destroyed the last of its kind in our county. Somehow Mother, as her own illness progressed, knew about the tree without being told. Now she will see, I thought. She has been wrong. You *can* give all of yourself away and have nothing left. Now these friends who came begging will stay away, *for they have at last taken all she had to give.*

Each night I prayed that God would send life back into its brown branches once again. "Not for me, Lord, not for the people or this county, but for Mother because she loved it!"

The hours were heavy as the rust on the hands of the courthouse clock. I waited for the mailman, waited for the time to give Mother her medicine, waited just to be waiting.

The dreaded day came when Mother was too weak to protest and had to stay in bed. I slept in her room on a cot that night; neither the answer to the riddle nor sleep would come.

In the morning I ran down into the garden, where hummingbirds chased each other from the honeysuckle to the early roses, and snapped the tree's branches. Surely, after all my prayers the night before, there would be a sign of life. But in my heart I knew it was dead forever.

I kicked up a loose brick from the path and threw it toward the fence. I was right; the scavengers had killed the tree. Mother had at last given away all she possessed.

When Dr. Lillie came that morning to see Mother, he didn't have to tell us what he found. I climbed the steps to my room on railroad-tie legs and closed my bedroom door.

"Oh, God," I argued. "She isn't good. Mother isn't good enough to come up there. She nags at me to get better grades. Butch, too. Never satisfied. She's always fussing at me to pick up my clothes and books. Don't you remember that she steals dirt from Shakamak? And don't you remember that she helped Mrs. Cain lie about Cam shooting his brother that night?" I tried to elaborate on all her faults. "She's not the kind of people you want in heaven, I'm sure!"

But I was sure of nothing.

About one o'clock that night I dozed off from exhaustion. Just before three I was awakened by a sound I could never quite identify. I tell myself that it was a wind blowing in the distance, yet not a leaf stirred on the trees outside Mother's window.

As if in answer to the question I could not answer, Mother moaned. I moved quickly from my chair to her side. "Did you want something?" I was eager, so eager to hear her speak.

"Baby? Is Butch okay?" I nodded. "Your dad?" I nodded again. How like her to worry even in her world halfway between heaven and earth.

"And you?"

"I'm fine."

Mother closed her eyes again and said, "That's good."

How could she say "good" at a time like this when my world was spinning apart?

The same sound of wind came again, but the leaves outside the window remained calm. I straightened my shoulders and went back to my chair.

A sound in the house below awakened me. Dad still slept upon the cot. Mother, too, was asleep. My watch said it was after five.

On numbed legs I stood up, turned off the lamp we didn't need, and tiptoed down the steps. On the kitchen table were fresh rolls. I recognized the plate they were on; it was one Mother had sent with a pie to the Cains' when Mr. Cain died the month before. Mrs. Cain couldn't afford to give to us. But she had, not asking for thanks; she had slipped away without awakening us.

I looked out through the kitchen windows toward the garden. As if God gave a signal the morning sun chose that moment to burst through its summer quilt of sky.

No knocks disturbed Mother that morning while Miss Dunn, my teacher, and other neighbors brought the best of foods and placed them on our kitchen table.

There are no words adequate to describe Genesis County working its miracles of love. Rachel Abel, the calico-skirted washerwoman, gathered our soiled clothes and returned them, ironed. Isaac Porter's widow did the dishes, helped clean the house, and explained, "Small payment for the time Bonnie sat up with my Timmy afore the Lord called him."

Grapes wasting on our vines came home in glistening, purple jelly glasses. Mr. Ishmael picked full-podded beans which his wife canned. Lot Ephriam dug potatoes and onions to fill the stonehouse bins. And best of all came Cosey Walters with a precious, so-hard-to-part-with African violet in her hand, the violet that was as dear to her as any child.

In spite of my grief, shame at ever doubting the love of these people covered me like sunburn in July. Then one morning Dr. Lillie came down the steps smiling.

"Best news I've had in a long time," he said as he fastened his collar. "We're gaining ground. Bonnie's count has been up now for the third day. Those shots every two hours last night are the answer."

Dad hugged me like the time I had been to 4-H camp for two weeks. Even Butch wore a smile and pecked at my cheek in a halfway kiss, making a face as if the taste was terrible. Joe, our black cocker, wagged his tail as if he too understood the good news.

"Was it the new medicine?" I asked, finding the news hard to grasp.

The doctor was putting pills into a tiny envelope as he turned to answer my question. "New medicine, Myra? The medicine that helped your mother is a higher power than anything I could have given her. One as old as time. So don't ask me any of your foolish questions, girl." He reached across to flatten my nose with his thumb, an old trick of his to make me look cross-eyed. "You see that she gets these, Redhead. I'll be back before noon. Could do with a little sleep myself."

If I could look back into my life and say that there was one moment when I grew up, it would be that moment. Dad ran up the steps to Mother's room with Butch and me and Joe at his heels.

It is said that a miracle takes only a minute, but to see Mother regain color in those few days was miracle enough for us.

"I'll be up soon," she promised on that third day as tiny pinpoints of moisture appeared on her upper lip. "I wonder," she asked Dad who stood beside her bed. She hesitated then, as if dreading the answer. "I wonder if you've had time to look after the Genesis Tree. Did it live?"

Dad looked down at his shoes for a split second.

"Oh, it di —" I began to explain.

"It's coming along okay," Dad interrupted me.

I spun around to search his face, for I had never heard him lie to Mother before.

The doctor was jubilant at Mother's progress. We knew her miracle was an answer to the prayers of the very people who had helped, in all innocence, to kill her Genesis Tree. Overflowing with love for her, they had brought their offerings, sent cards, and came visiting to cheer her. What she had given to them came back. Thus I knew that Mother's creed, that one can never give away all one possesses, was part of the riddle I had been trying to solve.

We looked forward to the next morning with joy. Dad helped her get out of bed. I waited down the hall in my bedroom.

From my favorite position, belly-bustered across my bed, I waited for her to come to look out from my triple windows to her beloved garden below.

Mother said nothing as she came on unsteady legs. I knew that inside she was breaking a twig on the Genesis Tree, snapping it between her fingers to be certain that life was forever gone from this momento of her family's past, still hoping to find life in it.

Dad stood close behind her as she looked.

"I wanted first to see my tree." Her voice still begged me to give her hope. "Did it live, Myra, honey? In fifteen years you've never lied to me about an important thing."

Dad shook his head to warn me. Again he interrupted. "Of course. Ailing, yes, but in the next spring, in the morning of its life, it will sprout again. Wait and see!"

Mother's smile traced the word RELIEF! in bold letters in the sunlight flooding into the room. She leaned for support on one of my bedposts and idly fanned the pages of my worn writer's notebook which was lying on my dresser.

The inevitable reckoning came.

"You see, Myra, I was right. Even if my tree, the last of its kind, dies, it proves that we cannot give away all we possess. The things I have shared with these wonderful people here in Genesis County came back to us in our need, didn't they? I was right."

Hating to be so humbled, I struggled to argue. Stubbornness made the answer choke in my throat like the tennis ball wedged into the gutter outside my window. She was waiting. Her hope and faith had survived all my stabs of doubt. Truth called upon me to judge. I wanted to say, "But you're wrong. They did kill your tree. They did! I'm right. Not you. No!"

The words I could not utter followed the wind out to the dead Genesis Tree; and when they echoed back to me, I knew what I had to say. "Yes, Mother, you were right."

There was a new proud note in her laughter then that made the yellow room a rainbow.

"And if your tree is dead . . . you will not be angry to know it?"

It seemed as if she had been wearing a heavy cloak and had been weighed down with it. Her voice lifted the cloak and tossed it aside.

"We cannot forever live in the past. It was George's tree in the first place, not ours. I borrowed it only for a little while and tried to share it when asked. But things have to die sometimes so that others may find a new way of life, or even life itself. Sometimes I know God planned it that way, for our thoughts, our loves, our trees, and yes, even your riddle, to remain unsolved until the day of judgment."

Then leaning toward me she spoke for all the ghosts of our family's past who had lived in this house. "Life, Myra, and the living of it is a wonderful thing! Now with so much to do, I must hurry to grow strong again."

I reached across from the bed to straighten my precious writer's notebook to keep it from sliding off the dresser. "It's so little," I said.

"Big enough, Myra. Words can make all of Indiana become a part of Genesis County and all of the world come to Indiana. Home is always home to everyone: it's something inborn in man . . . the longing. Choose to share it with your words. That is the only way to solve your riddle, for haven't you guessed by now that the answer to your riddle is within you? It's that way for everyone."

She was gone into the hall where Dad waited to carry her downstairs.

Joy was soaring inside me. The tall maples outside my windows filled with birdsong I had never heard before.

I had been wrong. And selfish. Giving was really all there was to the riddle of happiness. Living *was* giving, after all. Now I understood one of the sayings in my Johnny Appleseed book, for there it was written: "In death, what you have given you still have; what you have kept for yourself, you lose."

Mother's perfume lingered in my room as I drew the shades against the sun. My tears were not for myself. I had returned from walking into a far country only to find that the answer to the riddle of Genesis County was in the people I had always known.

I opened my precious Johnny Appleseed book once more to read the inscription the Fiddlin' Man had written on the flyleaf: *What creature is it that in the morning of its life . . . ?* I knew that I had read the riddle from the book for the very last time. The time of parting had come if I intended to grow up. The museum would be pleased with the gift of my book. And yet, it was not really like giving it away when I thought about how many people would enjoy looking at it. It was like sharing it — just as Mother had shared her tree.

I sat down to wait for the mailman to come. Had I really solved the riddle? Well, at least I had found some happiness, and that was a great clue toward the solution. Had I been the only one of my people who tried to find the answer to the riddle? No, there had been others like George Dillen Hawroth. And there would be more as long as life itself exists. Would anyone find a Genesis Tree alive again? Perhaps if I searched the woods of peoples' lives I would find one. I promised myself to try.

My riddle was really answered long ago by the old town crier when he stood beneath the first Genesis Tree at New Harmony, Indiana, and cried out the hour of midnight:

> Again a day is passed and a step made nearer the end.
> Our time runs away, and the joys of heaven are our reward.

But it is not midnight here. Here it is morning, the morning of my life, for I am young, and can search.